Y0-AES-679

ANIMAL ARK®

Kittens in the Kitchen

Ben M. Baglio

Illustrations by Shelagh McNicholas

SCHOLASTIC INC.

New York Toronto London Auckland Sydney
Mexico City New Delhi Hong Kong Buenos Aires

**Special thanks to Jerry Oldfield,
and to C.J. Hall, B.Vet.Med., M.R.C.V.S.,
for reviewing the veterinary information contained in this book.**

ISBN-13: 978-0-590-18749-7
ISBN-10: 0-590-18749-X

49 48 47 46 45 44 43 42 41 40   10 11 12 13/0

Printed in the U.S.A.   40
First Scholastic printing, May 1998

To Jenny Oldfield, who loves animals,
and to Peter and Benjamin,
the kittens in my kitchen

ANIMAL ARK

Where animals come first

®

One

"Mandy, you're very eager to get to school all of a sudden," Dr. Adam Hope said. He watched his daughter stuff old newspapers into her backpack. She flung on her school jacket, flicked a brush through her dark blonde hair, and snatched a mouthful of toast. "It's only ten to eight. Are you sure you're okay?"

"Very funny!" Mandy said. "Of course I'm okay. It's just a special day, that's all." She'd fed her rabbits and done her morning chores at Animal Ark. Simon, the nurse, had come in to look after the animals and take temperatures and give medicines. Now she was free to go.

"School trip?" Dr. Adam took a guess as Mandy unlocked her bicycle padlock and put on her bike helmet. He got no reply. "New boyfriend?"

"Ha, ha!" Mandy said. "No time now, Dad. I'll tell you later." She set off up the driveway, her long legs pedaling like mad. She waved at her mother.

"What's the rush?" Dr. Emily Hope rolled down her car window.

But Mandy had already sped by, under the wooden sign, "Animal Ark, Veterinary Clinic." She took one look back at the old stone cottage with its modern vets' extension to the rear, then she pedaled hard again.

"She's up to something," Mandy heard her mother say. "She's got that determined look on her face."

Mandy knew they wouldn't have a clue what she wanted with the old newspapers. But she ignored them and charged up the lane toward Welford village. She'd keep her mystery until evening, after her mother came back from her round of visits to the sick cats, dogs, goats, and hamsters that made up the busy practice of Animal Ark. She gave her mom and dad one last wave before she turned out onto the road. "See you later!" she yelled.

"This is it! This is the big day!" Mandy greeted her friend James Hunter. As usual, his straight brown hair flopped onto his forehead, and his glasses sat halfway down his nose.

"Hi," he said. "Do you realize I've dragged myself out of bed half an hour early to meet you outside this rotten store?" He was breathless from pedaling. "My dad nearly dropped dead with shock!"

"Come on!" Mandy said, ignoring his protests. "Let's go and see!"

Mandy and James rode their bicycles out of Welford on the two-mile stretch into Walton. Past all the sleepy cottages and wide-awake farms with their collie dogs at the gate, she never once stopped chattering.

"It's going to be today, I know it!" She had a feeling about these things. James nodded and panted to keep up. "I'm so excited I can hardly wait!" The ground sped by under their wheels. "She's been looking for a warm, dry place, and that's always a sign! Anyway, she refused her food yesterday." James nodded again in agreement. "I did see her on the custodian's porch yesterday after school, behind the stack of logs. She's a very smart cat!"

They pedaled down the final hill. Mandy's short hair blew back in the wind. The new one-story houses of Walton greeted them, spick-and-span. Walton Moor School lay behind the housing development, another new building that backed onto open countryside. Mandy and James rode through the gate into the deserted playground.

Mr. Williams, the custodian, strode through the yard, setting out parking cones for the garbage truck. It was Thursday, trash collection day. "Morning!" Mandy called, with James running to catch up. But Mr. Williams was a man of few words. He ignored her greeting.

"Shh, now!" Mandy warned James. They'd left their bikes locked up in the shed and came up behind the custodian's house. "We don't want to disturb her." Carefully they peered over the beech hedge, neatly trimmed by Mr. Williams. They scanned his pink rose bushes and the porch at the back of his house.

"Mandy," James dared to whisper, "does Mr. Williams know about this?" He was cleaning his glasses on his school sweater. "I mean, what will he say if he finds us snooping around on his porch?"

"He won't mind," Mandy whispered back. How could anyone mind about animals? "Mrs. Williams sometimes puts out food. I bet that's why Walton has chosen their porch to have her babies on!" Mandy's face shone with excitement.

"Walton?" James didn't realize the cat had a name. It was small, black and white, and rather ordinary. As far as he knew, it was a stray. But then,

Mandy had kept details about the cat pretty much to herself up till now.

"I named her after the school," Mandy said. "According to Mrs. Williams, she just turned up on the main doorstep one night, dumped inside a plastic bag with tiny airholes to breathe through. Can you believe it? People can be so cruel!"

Mandy could feel the prick of tears in her eyes even now. "She was only a young cat, and someone just dumped her!" She sniffed and tried to pull herself together. "She would've died if I hadn't come along early next morning and gone to the teachers' room for some milk for her. She was really neglected. I had to build her up." She squared her shoulders. "Anyway, that was six weeks ago. She's the school cat now, only a sort of half stray. So it's up to us to look after her!"

With that, Mandy eased open the back gate into the Williamses' garden. "Walton! Walton!" she coaxed, bending low and looking under the raised porch into the dark space there. James peered up onto the porch itself, behind the stack of logs. No cat.

"Walton!" Mandy called, a bit more loudly.

A black-and-white shape trotted across the long shadows of the lawn and over the flower bed; a round, heavy shape, nearly as wide as she was long, with a low belly. James spotted her first. "Mandy, look!" he said.

Mandy breathed a sigh. They'd gotten here in time. "Hello, Walton," she said. "Here's a nice, comfy place for you to give birth to your lovely kittens, see?" She climbed the porch steps. The cat followed. Mandy delved into her bag and pulled out the old newspapers. She showed them to Walton and let her sniff them. "See, nice and warm and dry!"

Then she and James banked up some of the logs to make a sort of den for Walton. They lined it with the newspapers, carefully overlapping them in thick layers. "See!" Mandy said again.

Walton brushed against Mandy's bare legs. She tilted her head up toward the special bed of logs and newspaper. Her delicate nose and whiskers seemed to approve, for she climbed, slow and heavy, up onto the ledge.

"It's in the sun, nice and warm," James said. "Good idea!" He grinned at Mandy, then blushed. In the distance, the morning bell sounded. "Was that the bell?" he asked clumsily. Then he shot off for homeroom before Mandy could reply.

"You hear that, Walton?" Mandy said. "That's the bell. I have to go." But she felt the strong pull that the cat had over her. Perhaps it was because she,

Mandy Hope, age thirteen, of Animal Ark, Welford, Yorkshire, England, was very like Walton, the school cat. They were both adopted. Her own parents had died in a car crash, too early for her to remember them, and Adam and Emily Hope had taken her in. Now she would do the same for Walton.

Softly she stroked the cat, then she caught hold of herself. "I'll stop fussing now and leave you to cope." She knew animals liked privacy at this time. "No one will bother you, and I'll be back later to see how you're getting along." Quietly she backed down from the porch, then quickly she cut across the garden, through the gate, and over the asphalt of the playground. The second bell had rung.

Mr. Williams, in his padded green vest, his old corduroy trousers, and his big laced boots, crossed paths with Mandy as she ran into school through the main door. As usual, he only grunted, head down and grumpy. Mandy thought it was best not to say anything to him about Walton and her arrangements for the birth. Leave it till later. Even Mr. Williams's heart would melt once he saw Walton's kittens nestling on his back porch!

Mandy rushed into class. She tried, and failed, to concentrate all the way through math, geography, and English.

* * *

At half past three James was waiting for Mandy at the lockers. "Ready?" he asked. Animals were the most important thing in James's life, too.

Dodging the crowds, they sprinted together up the slope to the custodian's house. Mandy could hardly breathe, she was so excited. This was Walton's big day!

"Walton!" Mandy called, opening the gate and crossing the lawn. They turned the corner up onto the porch. Mandy half closed her eyes. There Walton would be, tucked up in her newspaper bed, shielding her new kittens! She couldn't wait!

She opened her eyes. The bed was empty! Clean and dry and quite empty. Mandy looked at James. They felt the bottom of the world fall out.

"Where is she?" James gasped.

Mandy shook her head. "It's today. I'm sure it's today." She couldn't understand it. She'd seen enough cats giving birth to kittens at Animal Ark to know just how they looked when the great day came. Mandy and James stood on the porch, confused and alarmed.

"Listen!" Mandy said. The Williamses' back door stood open in the afternoon sunshine, and Mandy was sure she'd picked up a sound from inside. A tiny, high-pitched squeaking sound!

James stared at her. "What is it?"

Mandy stepped across the kitchen threshold. "Mr. Williams?" she whispered. "Mrs. Williams?"

The kitchen was neat and clean, scrubbed to perfection. Its lace curtains shone pure white. Its black-and-white tiles looked like an advertisement for floor cleaner. But it was empty. The squeaking noise was slightly louder. "In here!" Mandy said.

They tiptoed into the empty room.

"It's still very muffled," James said. He looked inside cupboards, trying to find the noise.

They looked under shelves, behind the vegetable bin, but still the noise escaped them.

"Walton!" Mandy called gently.

But Walton, wherever she was, didn't want company. Only the muffled, faint squeaking continued. Mandy followed it until she finally tracked it down.

There was a laundry basket in the corner of the kitchen, by the washing machine. It was an old-fashioned straw one with a lid. Mandy put her ear to it. The squeaking came from inside!

Gingerly she lifted the lid. It was dark and warm in there. The high-pitched noise rose to a wailing chorus. Mandy adjusted her eyes to the darkness and peered inside. She saw the black-and-white patches of Walton's fur; she saw the cat's eyes glint as she looked up. Obligingly, Walton lifted a paw and shifted sideways. "Look," she seemed to be saying, "four perfect kittens!"

Mandy could just make them out — four tiny curled-up things, gray and blind. Skinny, helpless creatures. She thought they were the most beautiful things she'd ever seen!

"Aren't they wonderful!" Mandy breathed, as James came to look over her shoulder.

He saw their blunt little faces and blind eyes. "Ye-es," he said. He clearly needed more time to get used to them.

"Oh, but they are!" Mandy cooed. She touched Walton gently under the chin. "Good girl!" she said. The kittens squeaked louder in protest at the light and the cooler air. Mandy gave in and replaced the laundry basket lid.

And then their luck ran out. Someone crossed the porch and filled the kitchen doorway. He was tall, bulky, and his feet made a noise across the wooden floor of the porch. "Amy?" he called. He paused, wiped his feet, then stepped into the kitchen.

"Mr. Williams! Um, hello!" Mandy said feebly. James stood alongside her, straightening his school tie, trying to look braver than he felt.

"What the heck!" Williams bellowed with shock.

"Amy! Where are you? What the heck!" he said again.

His wife came tottering through from the front room. She was slightly deaf, slightly nearsighted. "Don't shout, Eric," she sighed. "I can hear perfectly well without you having to shout!"

"Oh, can you?" her husband fumed. "I'll bet you heard these two prowling around in here perfectly well, too!"

Mrs. Williams sighed again. "Sit down, all of you," she said. "Everybody sit down while I make us a cup of tea!" It was clearly her cure for everything.

Mandy and James sat down as they were told, as far away from Mr. Williams as possible, while his wife made the tea. "Well!" he said over and over. "Can't a man even call his house his own anymore?"

"Oh, shush, Eric!" his wife said, giving him his favorite mug and a butter cookie. "Just give them a chance to explain!" She was little and skinny, half his size, but Mandy and James could see who was boss. "Well, then," Mrs. Williams smiled sweetly at Mandy. "I'm sure there's a perfectly good explanation!"

"There is," Mandy agreed. She looked wildly at James for help.

"The cat had kittens!" James blurted out.

"In your laundry basket," Mandy finished off.

"What!" Mr. Williams shot to his feet. He backed off into a corner.

"Wait!" Mrs. Williams went to investigate. She lifted the basket lid and peered inside. "It has," she confirmed calmly. "It had kittens, all right."

"On my best shirts!" Mr. Williams stammered. "It had kittens on my best shirts!"

"Calm down, Eric!" Mrs. Williams shook her head. "It's only a stray cat!"

"Only!" The custodian rolled his eyes in helpless anger.

"She won't do any harm," Mandy broke in.

"They've very clean animals. She won't leave any mess!" She tried to reason with him. "If you just leave her and the kittens there in peace for a few days, they'll soon be on their feet. Then you can make them a better place — a cardboard box, for instance. Just line it with newspaper and put it out on the porch. That should be fine!"

"A few days!" Mr. Williams repeated. His face seemed to be stuck. His mouth had dropped open; his eyes were bulging.

Mrs. Williams took Mandy and James aside. She shook her head. "It's no use. He can't stand them."

Mandy was slow to catch on. "Can't stand what?" Only now was she beginning to sense that there was a problem.

"Cats. He can't stand them. They set his nerves on edge."

Mandy breathed in deeply. How could people hate cats?

"He says they dig up his garden. He can't abide them." Mrs. Williams sounded sorry, but she sounded as if they'd just have to understand. Her husband was stubborn as a mule over cats. She turned and started clearing away the tea things.

"Just a few days!" Mandy said, dashing from one to the other. "We can't move them for a few days, in case the mother decides to abandon the kittens.

She might, if they get moved. Please let her stay where she is!" She felt breathless with fright, but she tried not to show it.

"Stay? In my laundry basket?" Mr. Williams snorted. "On my best shirts?" He tossed his head. "A load of smelly cats!"

"They're not —" Mandy interrupted, but James stopped her. He had a better idea of when to answer back than Mandy.

"Not likely!" Mr. Williams headed straight at Mandy and James to shoo them out of his kitchen. "Go on, you two. Get moving! I won't warn you again!"

Mandy and James backed off toward the door. Mr. Williams towered over them. "Please!" Mandy pleaded. She felt sick at heart.

"No!" Mr. Williams thundered. "They've got to go!" He glanced at his wife. "And there's no use you looking like that, Amy. I'm saying no, and I mean no!" He looked down at Mandy's terrified face. "I'm telling you once and for all, I'm not having them kittens in my kitchen!"

Two

Mr. Williams said his final word, then stormed out of the room. Tears sprang to Mandy's eyes. She looked in desperation at Mrs. Williams.

The old woman raised her eyebrows and rolled her eyes. She patted her neat gray hair. "Just give him a minute to cool down," she said. She lifted the laundry basket lid to take a peek for herself. "My, my," she murmured.

"He can't mean it," Mandy said to James, who was trying to drag her out of the kitchen onto the back porch. "He can't just sentence four perfectly harmless kittens to death, can he? It isn't fair!"

James shook his head and kept on pulling. "Come on, we'd better go!"

"Mrs. Williams!" Mandy pleaded.

The custodian's wife carefully washed the rose-patterned teacups. She put them away in a high, glass-fronted cupboard. "I'm saying nothing," she said steadily.

Mandy shook herself free of James. "But it isn't fair! I mean, what have those poor little kittens ever done to anybody? They deserve a chance to live, just like anyone else! You can't just chuck them away because they happen to have been born in an unusual place!"

"On top of my husband's best shirts," Mrs. Williams reminded her. "My Eric's very particular about his shirts." She turned to face Mandy, who was a head taller than she, but thin as a piece of string. "Anyhow, whoever said life was fair?"

"But if he moves them, they'll die! Walton will abandon them!" Again the tears pricked her eyelids.

Mrs. Williams stared up at her. "Walton?" She folded her arms and kept her gaze steady.

"The mother cat. I've called her Walton after the school. I wanted her to sound as if she belonged somewhere! As if she was looked after, and had a home, and somebody who cared!" Mandy rushed on.

The tears were rolling down her cheeks now. They ran with a salty taste into her mouth. She remembered the half-starved cat being dumped in the school doorway. She thought of herself. What would have happened to her if Emily and Adam Hope hadn't taken her in and cared for her when she was tiny?

"Mandy!" James whispered. "Don't cry. You see worse things than this at the Ark every day of the week, remember."

"No, let her alone," Mrs. Williams said thoughtfully. "She's right. They deserve a chance." She took Mandy by the hand and sat her down at the table. Late afternoon sun filtered in through the white net curtains. "But for goodness' sake, dry your eyes, young woman. I can hear my Eric coming back across the yard, and he can't abide waterworks!" She pulled a clean handkerchief out of her apron pocket and handed it to Mandy. "Quick, blow your nose!"

"Will you help us?" Mandy whispered. The custodian's big boots tramped up the steps and across the porch. "If you let the kittens stay, I'll come here every day, twice a day, to help look after them! I'll —"

"Shush!" Mrs. Williams warned. Her husband hung his cap on the door peg. She stood up and leaned forward evenly, with clenched fists down on the table.

"What the —!" Mr. Williams's face darkened as he caught sight of Mandy and James. "I thought I'd told you to clear out! What's the matter; are you deaf?"

"Now, Eric," Mrs. Williams began steadily.

"Don't you 'Now, Eric' me!"

"Now, Eric!" she insisted. "This young girl has been explaining to me again about these kittens being moved. It seems the mother won't have any more to do with them if we interfere. They have to be left alone."

A loud meow of agreement from inside the basket backed up the end of Mrs. Williams's firm speech. Thin squeaks followed after in a kind of chorus. Mr. Williams paced up and down the kitchen.

"Stand still, Eric, and listen!" Hands on hips, the tiny woman in the flowery apron confronted her heavyweight husband. "Where's the harm in it? You've got a drawer full of shirts up those stairs, most of them hardly worn. There's even one still in its package, pins and all — the one that your sister gave you last Christmas!" She eyed him sternly.

"You know I don't like shirts straight from the wrapping," he grumbled. "They're stiff and they itch!"

"I'll wash it." She didn't flinch. "Then you can wear it this Sunday to church, all right?"

Mandy held her breath. She had the good sense not to interfere in this argument, even though the little wailing sound from inside the basket was tugging at her heartstrings. James still stood sentry by the door, ready to escape.

Mr. Williams pointed an accusing finger at the basket. "My best blue shirt! My favorite!" he reminded her angrily. But it was the last trace of resistance. He knew when he was beaten.

"Now, Eric, it won't come to any harm. This young girl knows all about animals, don't you?"

Mandy nodded and gasped. "My mom and dad are both vets. In Welford, at Animal Ark!"

Mrs. Williams nodded, too. "See, she's a good girl. She promised to come in here twice a day to help look after those poor little things. They won't get under your feet. They'll just stay in there nice and cozy while Walton tends them."

"Walton?" Mr. Williams interrupted, looking curiously at Mandy.

"The mother cat," Mrs. Williams said, steady as ever.

"Crazy name for a cat," he grumbled, but he was definitely weakening.

"Well?" the fierce little woman demanded.

"Well . . ." He scratched his lined forehead with broad, work-worn fingers.

"All right, that's settled!" she said, like a suitcase snapping shut. "The girl will come in here each day until the kittens can begin to fend for themselves."

Mr. Williams grunted.

"That means yes," she reported to Mandy and James.

Mandy jumped up from the table, able to breathe at last. "Oh, thank you!" she said in a rush. "I'll go right away and get some food and extra vitamins and things for Walton. I'll be back as soon as I can. Walton will need lots of looking after, being such a small cat, and we may have to help her feed her kittens. I'll bring milk and a dropper just in case. She won't have that much milk herself, and four is a lot for her to feed, especially being so run down when she was a stray! We'll need to —"

"Whoa, hold your horses!" Mr. Williams backed off against the wall. "Not so fast." He turned to James. "Now listen, boy, maybe I can talk sense to you!"

James stood at attention, ready to listen.

"Man to man, I'm telling you straight. My wife, Amy, is too softhearted by far. Everyone knows that. And I've agreed to let those darn kittens stay put on top of my shirts because of her. I don't like it, but I want a quiet life. And when my wife makes up her mind about something, I generally give in."

Mrs. Williams smiled at Mandy, her hands clasped meekly in front of her.

"But," said Mr. Williams, "I just want to give your girlfriend here a word of warning."

Mandy saw James's face turn red at the word "girlfriend." But Mr. Williams thundered on.

"Now, I'm a mild-mannered guy, but before you both go running off for food and vitamins and whatever else, I want to make it clear that I won't put up with these smelly things camping out on my best shirts for a day longer than necessary, is that clear?"

James nodded. Mandy moved over to the door to stand beside him. They watched Mr. Williams's face take on the old angry look. "Quiet life or not, I'll give you just one week," he warned. "And that'll be that! After that, it's the end for the nasty little creatures!"

Mandy felt her heart go thump. She felt the blood drain from her face. "What do you mean?"

"I mean what I say. I'm giving you seven days. Find good homes for those kittens within the week, or else!" He stood with his feet planted wide apart, his face like a storm.

"Or else what?" Mandy gasped.

"Or else I'll deal with them myself!" He turned and stamped out of the kitchen, slamming the door after him.

James and Mandy flew back home on their bikes, up and down the hills to Welford. At the back of her mind hammered the horrible phrase "deal with them myself." Meaning what? Pictures of kittens drowning, hanging, being dumped in a sack by the side of a highway flashed through her head.

She yelled good-bye to James at the turn near the Fox and Goose tavern and hurried on up the road to Animal Ark. When she arrived, she threw down her bike in the backyard and rushed straight into the office.

"Mom!" she called. She dashed past Jean Knox in reception, who was busy signing out Miss Martin's Yorkshire terrier, Snap.

Jean looked up and smiled. "She's in the exam room," she said, but the door was already swinging shut.

"Mom!" Mandy slowed herself down and lowered her voice so as not to disturb the animals in their rows of cages and kennels.

"Hi, Mandy, over here!" Dr. Emily called. She had a blue-gray Persian cat up on the treatment table and was carefully feeling behind his left ear. She gave the cat a gentle stroke and popped him back in his carrier. "You're just about ready to go home," she promised. She turned to Mandy. "Now, what's all the drama?"

Her mom stood there in her white coat. She wore her long red hair tied back as usual, but it was always escaping. With her big green eyes and friendly face, Dr. Emily had the knack of calming Mandy down. "The school cat had four kittens," she reported.

"Ah!" Dr. Emily smiled. "That explains the newspapers. Good bedding for a birth. Did you get there in time?"

"Yes, but she didn't like the place on the porch that we'd fixed up for her." Mandy fiddled with the catch on the Persian's basket.

"No. They often don't." Dr. Emily hooked her thumbs in her coat pockets. "So?"

"So she gave birth in the custodian's kitchen instead."

"And?"

"And Mr. Williams, the custodian, hates cats!" Mandy looked at her mother with her wide blue eyes.

"Ah!" Dr. Emily settled back against the table. Dr. Adam came out of one of the treatment rooms to join them.

"Mo-om!" Mandy began to plead. "He's given us a week. We have to find homes for four kittens in a week. Otherwise he's threatening to take them off somewhere and put them down!"

Dr. Emily looked at her husband. "Hmm."

"It's not fair!" Mandy exploded. "He cares more about his stupid shirts than about the lives of four innocent animals! How can anyone be so mean?"

"Calm down, Mandy," Dr. Adam said. He was rubbing his beard thoughtfully. "What's this about shirts?"

Mandy explained. "Anyway, the kittens will be up and about in a few days, then it'll be okay to move them out of the stupid basket. Then he can have his rotten shirts back!"

"Mandy!" her mom warned. "Don't be rude. Some people just don't like cats, and you have to accept that." She lifted the cat basket and began to head for reception.

Mandy realized that her chance was slipping by. "Mom," she said, "can I take some milk and some vitamins back over there tonight?" She knew from watching her parents at work in Animal Ark what help Walton would need to feed the kittens.

"Of course," Dr. Emily nodded. She was already on her way out.

"And, Dad, can we take the kittens in here at the end of the week? Please!" Mandy sidled up to him.

"Ah!" Dr. Adam put an arm around her shoulder. He knew his wife was still listening. "Now, Mandy, you know our rules about that."

"I know, Dad, but this is different!" Mr. Williams was going to kill the poor little things if she couldn't find them homes!

"We don't take in strays, you know that. We're not a charity, remember. We're vets." Mandy guessed that it was a rule he might have bent a little. But his wife had a very firm business head. She came back toward them.

"The answer's got to be no, Mandy." Dr. Emily was kind but firm. She put the cat basket down and spoke gently. "Listen, the custodian has already done you a favor and given you a week, hasn't he?"

Mandy hung her head and nodded miserably. "It would only be for a while, Mom. We'd only have to have them for a while until Walton's finished feeding."

"Then what, hmm?" Dr. Emily glanced at her husband to check. "That's right, isn't it, Adam? We can't suddenly change our rule about strays. We'd be overrun with them in no time. You've got to understand that, Mandy."

Mandy nodded again. Her mom was always right,

but it hurt a lot to agree with her sometimes. She thought of the four helpless kittens being carefully licked clean by a proud Walton.

"Now, listen," Dr. Adam said in his cheerful voice. "Cheer up, this is a challenge!"

Mandy sniffed and looked up. "How do you mean?"

"You've got a whole week; look at it that way! One week to find four good homes for four furry bundles of fun. You can do it!"

She looked up at his lopsided, cheerful grin. "I can," she agreed. "Or rather, *we* can!"

"We?" her mom asked.

"Me and James."

"You and James!" her mom echoed, raising her eyebrows. "Well, then!"

Mandy ignored her. "Yes! Four homes for four kittens!" Mandy began packing sterilized droppers and vitamin drops in her pockets. "Easy. No problem!"

"Good girl," Dr. Emily said, satisfied.

Dr. Adam winked at his daughter. "That's my girl!"

Mandy was dashing about, back to normal. "I'll come up with a plan, just you wait!" She was out through reception, jumping on her bike, and pedaling up the driveway before her parents had time to draw a breath.

Back at school, Mrs. Williams opened the kitchen door to her and watched as Mandy carefully lifted the lid off the laundry basket.

"Hello, Walton," Mandy said gently. Inside the basket it was warm and dark. The cat purred up at her. "Come on, come and have some food!" She picked up the warm, soft cat and cradled her. The four kittens wailed miserably. "Sorry, but mother cats need looking after, too!" Mandy said as she closed the lid.

"There!" Mandy said as she set out milk and food on the kitchen floor for Walton. The cat arched her black-and-white back and rubbed against Mandy's legs. Then she settled quickly and daintily to her supper.

"Come and look!" Mandy whispered to Mrs. Williams. "Walton won't mind." Walton raised her head briefly as Mandy lifted the basket lid once more, then kept on lapping milk. They peered together into the dark nest. Clean and dry, the four kittens nestled on Mr. Williams's best blue shirt — blind and helpless, but quiet now — and snuggled against one another.

"Oh, my!" Mrs. Williams shook her head. "They look liked drowned rats!"

"No, they don't. They're beautiful!" Mandy whispered. "Look!"

"Well, at any rate they all look the same to me, all gray and furry and curled up like that."

"No, they don't. They're very different; can't you see?" And Mandy promptly decided to give them names. She picked them up, one at a time. "This one's Smoky, and this one's Patch." She looked carefully at the two remaining kittens, then grinned. "And this one's Amy. And this one's Eric!"

"Oh!" Mrs. Williams stood back, slightly shocked, then pleased in spite of herself. "Are you sure? I mean, I don't know what my husband will say!" She tut-tutted and smoothed her apron.

Mandy smiled and stood up as Walton finished her meal.

The cat leaped up into the basket, back on duty. She sprang down into the dark well, ready to let the kittens suckle. "I think we'll let her manage for now." She put the lid back on, testing it to make sure the cat could push it off easily by herself. "Maybe tomorrow we'll start giving the kittens extra milk."

"Hmm." Mrs. Williams nodded. "What time will you be back in the morning, then?"

"About eight o'clock. Before school starts."

The custodian's wife showed her out. "Make sure you don't forget!"

"No way!" Mandy waved, picked up her bike, and set off for home.

The sun was setting over the field as she rode past the new houses out onto the open road. The sky was pure red, the horizon dark brown. Mandy felt the wind. She was pleased with the day, happy that Walton had had such a good birth. She'd be a wonderful mother, even though she was so young herself.

Then Mandy's heart jolted. Smoky and Patch, Amy and Eric were all snuggled up for the night. There was a new world waiting outside for them, a big and dangerous place. Right now they were asleep. But Mandy tensed against the handlebars as she took the final curve down the hill into Welford. Her face frowned. She had a week to find four homes. Mr. Williams's threat lurched out of the lengthening shadows like a giant from a fairy tale. "Find good homes for them kittens within the week. Or else I'll deal with them myself!" he roared. Mandy knew he wouldn't relent. He meant what he said. A death sentence hung over the poor little kittens, and only she could save them!

Three

Dr. Adam glanced up from the television as Mandy wandered in. The living room was low, with wooden beams, a big stone fireplace, and cozy red-patterned rugs on the old stone floor. It was a cold evening, and a log fire crackled. "Got any home-work?" he asked.

"I've already done it." Mandy flicked through a magazine. She was frowning and restless.

Dr. Adam looked at her again. "Why not take that back to your grandmother's?" he suggested.

Mandy nodded. She was thinking, thinking; what to do to find homes for those kittens? But she picked up the little magazine and drifted off down the hallway.

"Where are you off to?" her mom asked as she came in through the front door. She'd just gotten back from her yoga class, relaxed and smiling as usual.

"I have to clean out the rabbit hutch, then I'm off to Grandma and Grandpa's," Mandy said absent-mindedly. She waved the magazine, still deep in thought.

"Say hello from me!" Dr. Emily shouted after Mandy, but she got no answer.

Mandy let Flopsy, Mopsy, and Cottontail out into the run in the backyard while she cleaned out their hutch and laid down fresh straw. Satisfied that their water was clean and that they were safely bedded down for the night, she set off up the lane to her grandparents' cottage.

In the cool evening light, the mass of white lilacs in her grandfather's garden gave off a strong, sweet scent. Even at this late hour he would be out in his greenhouse, puttering. "Hi, Grandpa!" she said with a wave. She stood to wait for him by the new camper sitting proudly in their side driveway.

"Hello, sweetie!" His face lit up, and he came out to greet her. He slid the greenhouse door closed.

"Come in, come in. Your grandma's inside writing letters."

He showed her in through the kitchen and into the cozy back room. The lamps cast a yellow glow and the flowered curtains were closed. "Hello!" Mandy's grandmother gave her a wide smile. "Guess what I'm doing."

Mandy sat down opposite her at the table. "Writing a letter?" She loved visiting her grandparents. Even when she felt down, like now, somehow they cheered her up.

"Not just any old letter!" her grandmother announced. "This one is special. This one is to the prime minister!"

"Oh!" Mandy tried not to sound too surprised. She was used to her grandmother knitting impossible cardigan patterns and making gallons of rhubarb-and-ginger jam, not writing letters to prime ministers. "What is it about?" she asked.

"It's about our post office. There are nasty rumors in the village that they want to close it down. Mr. McFarlane told me about it when I went in to pick up some stamps earlier today."

"Why do they want to close it?" Mandy couldn't imagine life in Welford without their little post office.

Grandma raised her glasses onto her forehead. "They say it's too expensive to run. Too expensive, I ask you! Honestly, they don't know what they're talking about! We have to stop them!"

"So Dorothy's writing to the prime minister. Always go to the top is what I say," Mandy's grandfather said. "On her best notepaper, of course!" He winked and handed her a glass of homemade lemonade.

"On my official notepaper. I'm writing as chairperson of the Welford Women's Club!"

Mandy looked impressed. Even the prime minister would have to listen to her grandmother when she was on her high horse. "They won't close the post office," she said. "Not after they've read your letter!"

They all chuckled. "You've spoiled my concentration," her grandmother said. She put pen and paper aside. She looked at Mandy's fidgety hands. "Anyway, you have something on your mind, I can tell."

Mandy didn't need a second invitation. The story of Walton and her kittens poured out — how she was the school cat, but Mandy felt she must take charge. How Mr. Williams had no heart at all. How she, Mandy, had to find homes for the kittens. Her grandparents tut-tutted and nodded in all the right places. Mandy paused at the critical point and took a deep breath. "Grandma," she said, trying to sound very reasonable, "I've been thinking."

"Yes?" Her grandmother gave her a sideways look.

"Well, I've been thinking that a cat would be the perfect thing for you here in the cottage. I mean, it's lonely this far up the lane, and you hardly see any neighbors, and a cat is really good company for . . ." She faltered and blushed.

"For old people?" Her grandfather finished the sentence. He grinned. He was sixty-five — a gardener, a walker, a bicycle rider. He was fit as a fiddle.

"Yes," she admitted. "Anyway, they're sweet, clean animals, and you don't have to fuss over them. They look after themselves, and —"

"Whoa!" her grandfather said. "Hold on!" He looked helplessly at his wife.

"Look, honey," her grandmother spoke gently. "It's a good idea, and it's very good of you to be thinking of us like this, it really is. You're our beautiful, warmhearted girl, you know that!"

Mandy saw a great big "But" looming on the horizon. "Yes?" she said, feeling her heart sink.

Her grandfather took over. "But we've just bought our camper. You know, our retirement treat!" He jerked his head sideways. "There she stands in the driveway all shiny and new, waiting to take us to the Italian Alps, to Provence, to Portugal!"

"To Scarborough, the day after tomorrow!" her grandmother put in.

Mandy nodded. "So?"

"So we won't be at home to look after a pet as much as we were when your grandpa was working. We'll be out on the open road, the freeway, with the wind in our hair and the sun on our faces!"

Mandy was shocked. She wondered if she'd ever see her grandparents again!

"Not all the time," her grandfather corrected. "I still need to keep an eye on my tomatoes!"

"But too much of the time to be able to take in one of your kittens," her grandmother said finally.

And Mandy had to accept that. Smoky was the one she'd been planning for them to have, with his perky face and his way of pushing the other three kittens out of the way when they were feeding. Now Smoky wouldn't be sunning himself on her grandfather's patio after all. Mandy tried to swallow her disappointment.

"But . . ." her grandmother said, sweeping stray hair up into the bun at the back of her head, "we can still help!"

"How?" Mandy leaped at the promise. Her eyes lit up.

"We'll help you look for homes. How many kittens are there? Four?" Grandma got on her thinking cap. "There's Eileen Davy at the Old School House, but she's on the main road, and she's already lost two cats to the traffic, poor things. There's Myra Hugill, but she has to look after her sick sister in York right now. There's Dora Janeki from Syke Farm, but she's a loony old thing, and her new husband isn't known as an animal lover."

Mandy seized each name, then let it drop as her grandmother counted them off on her fingers. She was beginning to feel hopeless again.

"Wait!" her grandfather said. "I've just had a brilliant idea!"

Mandy swung around to face him. "What?"

"The post office!" he said, raising a finger.

Mandy looked puzzled. "Not right now, Grandpa. We're talking about Walton's kittens!"

"I know. That's why I mentioned the post office. That's my brilliant idea!"

"Oh, I see!" her grandmother said. "Yes, Tom, of course!"

"What? What?" Mandy didn't see at all.

"The bulletin board in the post office! That's what!" Her grandpa took a postcard out of the bureau and uncapped his old fountain pen. "Watch."

He wrote in beautiful old-fashioned letters:

WANTED!
FOUR GOOD HOMES
Cat lovers needed to provide
homes for kittens.
Please call Welford 703267.

"There!" he said, standing back and looking at his work of art. "You can take it down to the post office first thing in the morning."

Mandy took the sign. She nodded and smiled. "Brilliant, Grandpa!"

He screwed the top back on his pen. "It's nothing, my dear," he said modestly.

"Yes, it is, it's brilliant! We'll get millions of calls, you'll see!" Welford was full of animal lovers, and this was the perfect way to find them. Everyone went into the post office at some time during each day. Mandy hugged both her grandparents.

"Maybe not millions," her grandmother advised.

"All right, dozens!" Mandy said, laughing at her own habit of exaggerating. They all laughed together.

She left the house, smiling and happy. She closed

the gate with its Lilac Cottage sign, waved, and set off down the lane. Tomorrow was Friday. She'd be at the post office first thing in the morning. She'd spend the weekend answering all the phone calls. She ran home full of plans and preparations.

Mandy had arranged to meet James again to go to school early. She'd already been into the post office and pinned up her "Wanted" sign right in the center of the bulletin board. She greeted him cheerfully with, "You're seven minutes late, James Hunter!"

James pushed his glasses back onto the bridge of his nose. "Sorry," he said. He screeched to a halt on his bike. "I had to walk Blackie. Dad's away. And then I had to feed Benji."

"Oh, well, then," Mandy forgave him. Being late because of a dog and a cat was quite understandable. "Let's go!"

They made up some time on the journey. Traffic was still light, and they knew all the back ways. By five past eight they were knocking on the Williamses' kitchen door.

Mrs. Williams opened it with a worried face. "I thought you weren't coming! Come in, come in," she said.

"Is something wrong?" Mandy was unpacking cat food and a carton of milk on the kitchen table.

"I'm not sure. It's too quiet in there for my liking. Not like yesterday with all the racket. Even Eric noticed." Mrs. Williams watched anxiously.

Mandy lifted the basket lid. "Hello, Walton!" she said. But the cat lay on her side and only managed a feeble meow. "Leave me in peace," she seemed to say. She raised her head, but she didn't stretch and make her way out into the daylight to get some breakfast.

"Poor thing, she's exhausted!" Mandy said. "James, you'd better open that can of food. I'll lift her out." She reached in, tenderly lifting the tired cat. "She'll be all right in a minute," she told Mrs. Williams. She knew from helping out at home that there was nothing seriously wrong. "She just needs a little extra care." And she set the cat down to feed.

Walton wobbled, steadied herself, and eagerly got to work on the dish of meat.

"What about the kittens?" James said.

Mandy cast an expert eye over the four huddled shapes. "Fine!" she said. "But we'll have to feed them. We'll need the droppers. And we'll have to use the ordinary milk for now." She'd seen her mom and dad do it often enough. Now she hoped she could manage it all by herself.

James got the droppers from her bag. Mandy

gently heated the milk. Then she lifted one of the featherlight bundles. She sat with it on her lap and eased open its tiny mouth. "Come on, Patch, come on!" she coaxed.

She squeezed the rubber bulb of the dropper and took in milk from the warm pan. Then, while she held open the kitten's mouth with two fingers, she eased the glass tube between its lips with the other hand. She squeezed again and watched Patch's tiny tongue lick and then swallow the liquid. "See?" she said to James. "Now you try it."

He nodded and took another kitten, Smoky, out of the basket. Afraid but determined, he copied Mandy's actions with a second dropper. Smoky looked surprised, then gulped. James looked up in triumph.

"All right!" Mandy said.

It was fifteen minutes later and they were just finishing with the last two kittens when Mr. Williams tramped back in from unlocking the school. James and Mandy were busy stroking the kittens' throats to encourage them to swallow. Mr. Williams heard the tiny mewing from the basket. "What's up with the mother cat?" he barked.

"Tired out," Mrs. Williams said. "And you would be, too." She hovered by the sink like a worried relative.

"Hmm." He turned back out of his kitchen, grumbling.

"This place is being turned into a cat hospital! A man can't even call his home his own anymore!"

Mandy and James finished the feeding and cleaned up the room to perfection. Walton was sitting on the step, in the morning sun. She gave herself a thorough licking. Mandy bent to stroke her. "Good girl," she said. She was relieved when Walton decided it was time to return to her kittens. They watched her walk across the shiny tiles, jump up, and nimbly lift the basket lid with one paw. Then she disappeared from sight.

"Smart cat!" James said. He looked at his watch. "It's a quarter to nine," he reminded Mandy.

They said a hurried good-bye to Mrs. Williams and ran out through the garden and across the playground. A strong wind blew white blossom petals diagonally across the pavement. "What do you think?" James asked, pausing before they passed under the great stone arch of the main entrance.

"Oh, Walton will be all right," Mandy said. "She'll just have to take things easy." She hitched her backpack higher onto her shoulders and brushed cat hairs off her navy blue skirt. "But I'm not so sure about the kittens now."

Mandy didn't want to scare James, but she

thought the cat's milk might dry up. This sometimes happened when the mother wasn't strong. If
so, the tiny things would soon starve to death.
"We'll have to wait and see. Perhaps Walton will be
able to go on feeding them herself."

"What if she can't?" James wanted to know.

Mandy thought of the kittens with their gradually
opening eyes, their fluffier coats, their attempts to
struggle up onto all fours. They still tumbled and
collapsed like rag dolls. She could hold them easily
in the palm of her hand. "Well, we'll just have to
keep on feeding them ourselves," she said.

All morning long Mandy had kitten worries on
her mind. There was the old one of finding four
good homes in less than a week, and the new one
that she wouldn't confess even to James. But the
question kept crowding in on her. It wouldn't go
away. Walton was exhausted from the birth. The
kittens were clinging to life by a thread. And the
question still whirled in her head as Mandy sat and
ate her packed lunch in B Hall with Kate and
Melanie: Would they need to find homes for the
kittens after all? Would the poor little things even
survive?

Four

Mandy decided that the best answer to her question was a great big "yes!"

You have to think "yes" all the time, or life will get you down, she told herself. She and James would hand-rear the kittens if necessary. So she set about finding homes for them with even more energy than before.

She and James fed Walton and the little gang of kittens right after school, then they rode their bikes back to Animal Ark. "We're going to make more signs!" Mandy announced. She led James upstairs and rummaged under her bed, looking for some neon-pink poster board she'd stored there before

Christmas. "Then we'll be sure that every single person in Welford will read one!"

She liked to work in her room; it was an art gallery of animal posters. Horses and rabbits, dogs and cats stared down from her walls. Hardly an inch of wallpaper showed through, just how Mandy liked it. Mandy and James knelt on the floor to cut out small rectangles of pink cardboard. They chose broad black felt-tips and began designing their own signs. "Where will we stick these?" James wanted to know.

"Shh, I'm thinking!" Mandy said. She wanted eye-catching words to draw people's attention. Finally she wrote in big capital letters:

KITTENS IN THE KITCHEN
Bring love into your life.
Cats make cozy companions.
Adopt a kitten. Call Welford 703267.

It was catchier than her grandfather's sign. She was pleased as she knelt back to judge the effect, while James finished his much more practical notice:

HOMES NEEDED FOR FOUR KITTENS!
Remember, pets are for life!
If interested, call Welford 703267.

"I could put this one on your board in reception," he suggested.

Mandy nodded. "Good idea. Let's go down and ask Jean before she leaves for the day." She knew Jean liked to know exactly what went up on the bulletin board in reception.

They went downstairs and through the house into Animal Ark. Jean had closed the appointment book and was searching for her car keys. She had been their receptionist for five years and she was always losing her keys. Mandy knew all the places they were likely to be. She began helping Jean search.

"Here they are!" Mandy lifted the blue book and handed the keys to Jean.

"Oh, silly me!" Jean said, as she always did. She wore her glasses on a silver chain around her neck and still managed to forget where she'd put them.

James tried not to smile. "Can we put a 'Homes Wanted' sign on your board, please?" he said.

Jean took the sign, looked for her glasses, found them hanging down around her neck, and read the words. "That looks fine. Just find a space over there beside all the others," she said.

"Others?" James looked at Mandy. They scrambled across to the board. In the bottom corner there were at least six other "Homes Wanted" signs. James and Mandy's faces fell a little.

"Only three of them are for kittens," James said. Two others were for puppies, one for a pony.

Mandy counted up quickly. "Yes, but that's fourteen kittens needing homes altogether!" Fourteen kittens in a tiny place the size of Welford.

"Come on, chop-chop!" Jean said. She was busy locking cupboards, windows, drawers, and anything else that stood still. "I want to shut up shop!"

They looked again at the signs, trying not to feel downhearted. "Ours is the brightest one!" James said. "And it's in the best place!"

Mandy agreed. "I have another idea!"

With the second bright pink card in her hand they shot off ahead of Jean, up the driveway, and down into the village. "It's Friday. Grandma will be playing badminton!" They rode on past the post office and the general store toward the village hall.

"So?" James overtook Mandy. His soccer training was coming in handy for stamina. They headed for the village hall, which was set back from the road, next to the church.

"They have a Women's Club bulletin board in the entrance," Mandy reminded him.

"Right." James nodded and kept up the pace. Lots of kindhearted ladies came to the village hall to do flower arranging and cake icing, besides the Friday evening badminton club. It was a great place for one of their signs.

They almost bumped into Miss Davy from the Old School House as she came out of the hall, racket in hand, and not a silver-blue hair out of place. She turned and called in a shrill voice, "Dorothy, one granddaughter!" She smiled at them and continued on her way.

Grandma emerged, red-faced and breathless. She wore a bright turquoise track suit. "Mandy!" She gave her a quick peck on the cheek. "How nice. But it's thirteen-eleven, final game. I can only spare a second!"

"Sorry, Grandma." Mandy held up her KITTENS IN THE KITCHEN sign. "Can we pin this on the bulletin board?"

Mrs. Hope squinted at it. "Oh, the kittens? Yes, yes, of course. Good idea. 'Bye, honey!" And she dashed back to finish her game.

Mandy opened the glass door of the bulletin board and made space between lists of flower arrangers for the church, dates of Brownie meetings, and a charity drive. She pinned her sign firmly in the center, closed the door, stood back, and admired it.

"That should do it!" James said.

They were pleased with the evening's work as they finally said good-bye and headed home.

After supper Dr. Adam took Mandy into Animal Ark with a secret smile on his face. "Come and see a new admission," he invited.

Near the door of the residential unit was one of the see-through cages, shaped like a cat carrier but made of clear plastic. Dr. Adam picked it up.

"What is it?" Mandy could see the usual newspaper nest and a roll of soft gray cloth, but she couldn't spot any animal in there.

"Squirrel!" her father said. A small black nose peeped out of the newspapers. "A baby. Five weeks old." Two large black eyes appeared, and out it came, the size of a hamster, with a long, long tail. Dr. Adam unlatched the cage door and lifted it out. He handed the little gray squirrel to Mandy.

"Oh!" she said. She was speechless with delight. She felt its sharp little feet. She stroked its soft gray back, while the baby tried to suck the end of her finger. "Where's its mother?" she asked.

"She got run over."

Mandy gasped, and her face crumpled.

"Yes, I know," he said, looking at her. "And this little one would have died if someone hadn't found him."

Mandy shook her head. Life could be so cruel.

"You'll never guess who brought him in."

"Who?"

"Old Ernie Bell from the cottages behind the Fox and Goose."

Mandy looked surprised. She knew Ernie Bell as a grumpy, silent old man who shuffled down the village street with his bag of groceries.

"He came in and handed him over. ''Ere, veterinary,' he says to poor Jean, 'just check 'im over while I fix up a run for 'im in my backyard. I'll be back for 'im in twenty-four hours. Just check 'e's all right!' And he leaves the little fellow with Jean and stomps off to build a wire netting run. Who'd have believed it?" Ernie didn't have the reputation of being soft on animals. Dr. Adam put the baby back in its cage.

"What's the roll of cloth for, Dad?" Mandy bent down to study the squirrel in his cage.

"For comfort; something for him to snuggle up to. Animals need a mother substitute, you know. Something to take the dead mother's place." His voice was warm. He put an arm around Mandy.

"What are you feeding him with?"

"This stuff. It's the bottle food we give to orphan kittens. Why?"

Mandy was making new plans for Walton's

brood. She took the box of white powder and read the list of ingredients and instructions printed on the side. "Can I buy some of this from this week's pocket money?" she asked.

"For your school kittens?" Dr. Adam lifted three boxes down from the shelf. "Go on, take them. You don't have to pay!"

Mandy smiled. "Walton's a little weak right now. We'll have to help her feed the kittens properly."

"Well, this stuff is much better than cow's milk," Dr. Adam said, adding an extra box. "Mix it with boiled water, and use these little bottles with rubber nipples. The kittens can suck these properly. Everything's sterilized, of course."

"How often?" Mandy realized that there was a proper way to do this. The kittens' lives depended on it.

"Every couple of hours for the first week."

Mandy gulped.

"Less if the mother cat can still give milk herself, during the night for instance."

"I think she can. She's just a very small cat, and she's tired." Mandy was still determined to think the best.

"Well, then, this stuff four times a day will do the trick. Breakfast, lunch, after school, supper." He glanced at Mandy's serious face. "You're going to be busy," he said. "Any luck with finding homes for them yet?"

"Not yet." She bent thoughtfully to the level of the baby squirrel in the cage. "Will Mr. Bell have to let him go eventually, back into the wild?"

Her dad shook his head. "He's not allowed to. It's against the law, I'm afraid. That's because he'd never survive out in the wild now. Poor little fellow, it seems he'll have to make do with Ernie's backyard for the rest of his life!"

Mandy nodded.

"Don't worry, there are worse fates," Dr. Adam said.

"Oh, I know." But Mandy was still in a serious mood as she rode over to school with the special kitten food. True, like Ernie Bell and the little squirrel, she was giving the kittens a chance of life. But without homes, would it be a life worth living?

She rode and prayed that the signs in the post office, Animal Ark, and the village hall would work. She wondered, too, whether she could persuade Mr. Williams to give them more time. A week was so short! She leaned her bike against the hedge and went up the steps into the custodian's kitchen.

* * *

Once Walton was happily eating, Mandy showed Mrs. Williams the new arrangements for Smoky, Patch, Amy, and Eric. To her surprise, the custodian's wife actually offered to help. "Don't tell my husband!" She pressed her thin lips tightly together. "He wouldn't approve!" She took Amy out of the basket and gingerly snuggled her up against her flowered apron, complete with feeding bottle. "Poor little scrap!" she murmured.

Mandy smiled. "She's fine. Look, she's hungry!"

Mrs. Williams sat happily when the kitten fed. "You mustn't mind my Eric," she confided. "I know, he must seem like a grumpy old nuisance to you, but he's not so bad, really."

"No." Mandy tried to believe it. All she could think of were Mr. Williams's big boots and his loud voice. Hands as big as shovels. Temper like a volcano.

"You must think he's a stubborn old mule."

"No!" Mandy knew she didn't sound sincere.

"Yes!" Mrs. Williams looked down into the kitten's face. "Yes, you do. But he loves his garden!" She bent sideways toward Mandy. "Do you know, he keeps a squeeze bottle full of water out there on the porch. If a cat comes anywhere near his roses looking as if it's going to dig, Eric pulls out the bottle. You should hear him when he scores a direct hit!"

"One wet cat!" Mandy joined in the laughter. "I was thinking he might give us a little longer than a week," she said. "Even when we find homes for the kittens, Walton will have to go on looking after them for quite a while. The less we need to move them around the better." She looked pleadingly at Mrs. Williams. "Maybe you could persuade him?"

"Hope by name, hopeful by nature!" Mrs. Williams said. But she was shaking her head. "No, I know Eric. He's made up his mind!"

"Can't you just try?" Mandy was busy cleaning up the bottles and saucers.

But this time Mrs. Williams wouldn't bend. "No, it's not fair to him. He won't come into his own kitchen as it is. I know, I know," she interrupted Mandy's protest, "it's not sensible. But Eric's not always a sensible man. Who is? I'll tell you something else. He has a lot of pain, bending and kneeling and such. Arthritis. In the knees. Very painful." She lowered her voice. "To tell you the truth we don't mention it in case the school happens to hear. He's worried about his job!"

Mandy nodded. Suddenly Mr. Williams seemed human after all. "I'm sorry to hear that."

"Well, don't say I told you," Mrs. Williams warned. They were standing out on the porch. Walton was perched on the rim of the laundry basket licking herself clean. "He's out playing darts this evening. It cheers him up."

Mrs. Williams stared up at the pebbled clouds. "But Eric's a worried man. It's the job, the house, everything. And the pain, of course. I can't even get him to go to a doctor." She glanced at Mandy. "So, you see, I can't ask him to do any more, can I? He's done enough already."

Mandy agreed and smiled sadly. She rode home slowly. She understood more about Mr. Williams's bad temper now, that was certain. But it didn't stop time passing. The sand was running steadily through the hourglass. They had five days left!

Five

"Hello, Welford 703267?" a woman's voice asked.

"This is it!" Mandy yelped, then lowered her voice to speak into the phone. "Yes, this is Welford 703267." She held her breath. "Who's speaking, please?" She gave her mother a hopeful thumbs-up sign.

"Hello?" The voice sounded shy and cautious. There was a long pause.

"Hello, this is Amanda Hope. Who's speaking, please?" Mandy made a face of pretend panic at her mom.

"Hello, I want Welford 703267." The voice

seemed strange and not used to talking on the tele-phone.

"Can I help you, please?" Mandy said firmly. What was going on here? Her mom had paused over the washing up and was trying to listen in.

"Did you put a sign in the post office?" the woman on the end of the phone asked. "Are you the person with the kittens?"

"I am!" Mandy said with a grin. "I take it you're looking for a kitten?" Dr. Emily winked and contin-ued washing the breakfast dishes.

There was a long, crackly pause. "My name is Miss Marjorie Spry. I live at The Riddings. Please come to see me at two o'clock precisely."

Then the phone went dead.

"Well?" Dr. Emily said.

Relief swept over her as Mandy realized that their plan was beginning to work. It was only nine o'clock on Saturday morning, and they'd already gotten a response! "Yes!" she yelled, nearly jumping for joy. "I'm going over to tell Grandpa!"

"Mandy, what if there are any more phone calls?" Dr. Emily was drying her hands, following her out.

"Write down the numbers on that pad, will you, Mom? I'm so thrilled I can hardly wait!" She rushed up the lane without a jacket. It was drizzling, but she didn't care.

Her grandparents were stacking cans of soup inside the tiny cupboard aboard their camper. "Tomato, minestrone, cream of chicken!" Her grandmother handed them up to her grandfather and ticked them off her list.

"Can opener?" Her grandfather popped his head out of the sliding door. He saw Mandy. "Hello, sweetie!"

"It worked! It worked!" she greeted them. "Your brilliant sign, Grandpa, it worked!"

He rubbed his hands. Mandy's grandparents both stood there in their twin knit sweaters, the drizzle wetting their gray hair. "It has? You have a response then?"

"Of course she has a response, haven't you, Mandy?" Grandma put in. "Come inside. We're all getting wet."

"Who is it?" her grandpa asked as he put on the kettle. "Anyone we know?"

"It's someone called Spy. No, Spry. That's it, Miss Marjorie Spry!"

Grandma shut the kitchen door firmly and wiped her feet. Her head went to one side. "The Riddings, right?"

"Yes, The Riddings. Why, what's the matter? Do you know her?"

Her grandmother straightened herself up and bustled with the cups and saucers. "Yes. She lives at the big house out on Walton Road. Set back from the road. You know, the big old house."

"I know!" Mandy said. They passed it every day on the way to school. It was well away from the traffic, with a huge lawn and garden. The perfect place for a cat to live! "She wants me to go and see her there at two o'clock this afternoon."

"Does she now?" her grandmother said. "That'll be one for the record book!"

"Why? What do you mean?" Mandy was nearly bursting with impatience. "I thought you'd be pleased!"

"We are, sweetie," her grandfather soothed.

"They don't usually like visitors, that's all," Grandma explained. "In fact, I believe the last person they had over their threshold was Mr. Lovejoy, the old pastor before Mr. Walters, and that must be over five years ago!"

"No!" Mandy couldn't believe it.

"Yes, when their father died, the two sisters went into a sort of hibernation. It's true!" Grandma insisted. "Still, that won't make any difference to you,

I don't expect. If Miss Marjorie Spry wants to see
you about a kitten, and she's asked you to come
over, you go see her." She patted Mandy's hand.
"They're harmless. A bit peculiar, but harmless
enough."

"Anyway, it's best to check these places before
you send these precious kittens off to their new
homes," her grandfather agreed. "You have to see if
they're the right sort of thing!"

Mandy nodded, but she refused to give up hope. ·

"Take someone along with you," her grandfather
suggested. "Just to be on the safe side."

"James will come with me," Mandy said. She
lifted a cardboard box full of bread, cornflakes,
milk, and margarine. "Where do you want me to put
these?"

Together they finished packing for "the great trial
run," as her grandfather called it. He meant their
first expedition in their new camper. Finally they
were ready.

"Map?" Grandpa said, climbing into the driver's
seat.

"Map!" Grandma produced it from the glove com-
partment.

He turned on the windshield wipers. "Rubber
boots? Raincoats? Rain hats?"

Grandma flipped the map at him. "Ready?" she laughed. They waved to Mandy. "To sunny Scarborough!" she cried.

Mandy watched them disappear into the drizzle. There were still four hours to go before the visit to The Riddings. She would call James to arrange to meet him, then fill up the morning with little jobs at Animal Ark, and of course by riding over to feed Walton and the kittens.

Two o'clock came at last. They arrived to find the front lawn of The Riddings spread out like a soccer field. James and Mandy decided to leave their bikes at the gate.

"I wonder who cuts this grass?" James said. It went in neat strips, light and dark. The edges were neatly clipped.

"I do!" An ancient man in corduroy trousers growled at them from behind a laurel hedge. He was bent almost double, probably from years and years of clipping the edges of huge lawns, Mandy guessed. "Have you come about a kitten?" he growled again.

They nodded.

"Miss Marjorie warned me about it. 'Geoffrey,' she said, 'show the girl up to the door!' So I'm following orders. This way!" He trudged ahead of them up the gravel driveway.

The house was as big as a hotel, built of stone, with pointed towers at each corner. It was covered in ivy. Though they passed it every day, James and Mandy could truly say that they'd never really paid much attention to it before. It had arched windows, stone pillars, and massive steps up to a wide front door. "Like a setting for a horror film!" Mandy whispered nervously.

Just when they felt they needed him most, their guide left them. "This is as far as I ever go. Ring three times," he said. "Nice and loud, now. You might have to wait." And he went off, bowed and grumbling, to mow the lawn.

They looked at each other, shrugged, then James rang the bell. Silence. He rang again. And again. Finally someone began rattling locks on the other side of the massive door. "Wait!" a tiny voice ordered.

"What do you think we're doing?" James whispered to Mandy, trying not to laugh.

"Shh!" Mandy said. They had to be on their best behavior.

But even Mandy couldn't stop her jaw from hanging wide when the door finally creaked open.

The hall was the size of a ballroom, all in pink marble, with dark wood panels and glass chandeliers. But it was dull with age and gray with years of neglect. What had once been as splendid as a fairy tale had now decayed.

"Yes?" A lady stood before them. Her sticklike arms and legs poked out from the moth-eaten cream silk robe. She peered at them like a bat in the light.

"Miss Spry?" Mandy said uncertainly. A loud voice would have knocked the old lady down flat, she was sure.

"Yes!" She blinked her watery gray eyes. A skinny hand clutched the neck of her robe. "We don't see visitors!" she chattered.

Mandy's grandmother had been right. No one had come to this place for years. Curtains were closed to keep out the daylight. A collection of old blue-and-white china ornaments cluttered the windowsills. Great piles of yellow newspapers were heaped on shelves. "Miss Marjorie Spry?" Mandy repeated, her heart sinking as her eyes took in the mess.

"Joan! I'm Joan!" the woman shrieked. She began to close the door in their faces, but it was big and heavy. They saw the figure of another thin little woman come hurrying downstairs.

"Come in, come in," this second person ordered in a thin voice. She was beckoning to them, half running across the hall. "They've come about the kitten, Joan. Now open the door at once!"

And there they stood, two ladies thin as sticks, wild-haired, in matching silk robes. They had the same sharp face. They had movements that mirrored each other and voices that echoed and mocked. Identical twins! Miss Joan and Miss Marjorie Spry!

"We don't want visitors!" the first one, Miss Joan, repeated with a birdlike twitch of her head.

"Yes, we do. I invited them!" Miss Marjorie argued. "I want a kitten for this dreadful old place. I want to bring some life in here!"

Miss Joan stared stubbornly, silently back at her sister. Her hand stayed poised to slam the door shut.

"I do, Joan! I'm tired of living in this old museum of a place. I want some life. We're not old yet; let's make a fresh start!" Miss Marjorie pleaded. "Look, this girl is advertising kittens. So let her in!"

At last Miss Joan gave way. Fascinated, Mandy and James stepped inside. To them it seemed like actually stepping into the past, into a kind of prison. Miss Joan pushed the door closed after

them. It shut with a dull, heavy click. "What kittens?" Miss Joan challenged. She looked her sister in the face. "Who told me anything about a kitten?"

"I told you!" Miss Marjorie snapped. "The sign in the post office. Welford 703267!"

"But I don't like kittens!" Miss Joan protested. "You know that!"

Mandy stood in the middle of their argument, her heart sinking right into her shoes by now. Miss Joan would never give in over this. Anyway, who'd want to leave a kitten where it wasn't wanted one hundred percent by everyone in the house? She looked at James and could tell that he thought the same. They both sighed.

They watched as Miss Marjorie grew more and more angry. "How do you know you don't like kittens?" Her eyes seemed to spark. "Have you had one? Have you ever owned a cat in your entire life? Have you? Have you?"

She turned to face Mandy and James, smoldering with rage. "*I* like cats! Joan likes cats, though she says she doesn't! She only says it to be difficult. Yes, you do!" she snapped at her twin. "She's just a spoilsport. It's because it's *my* idea to bring a kitten to The Riddings, to help bring the place back to life a bit. She says no to all my ideas!" She nearly cried with exasperation. The tiny twins stood face to face like featherweight boxers.

"Anyway, I'm the older twin!" Miss Marjorie said grandly. "And I have decided. Don't listen to her!"

"Well, they're still very young," Mandy began to explain. "We're only trying to find suitable homes for them in the future, you see." Still she couldn't settle those doubts about this being a good place to bring one of her precious kittens.

"Where is it?" The older twin began poking at Mandy and James as if a kitten might be hidden in one of their pockets.

"She's still with her mother. We're just starting to look, as I said."

"Not here? You haven't brought it with you?" Miss Marjorie said sharply.

"Ha, ha, ha!" Miss Joan sang out. She did a little dance of delight. "Ha, ha, ha!"

Miss Marjorie's thin patience finally snapped. "Quiet!" she bellowed. She picked up an old black umbrella from the stand and launched it like a javelin at her noisy sister. It missed by miles, but Miss Joan froze on the spot. Then she grabbed a newspaper from a shelf and rolled it up like a base-ball bat. James and Mandy stood with their mouths open. Who would believe this?

"Joan!" Miss Marjorie warned.

"You threw something at me first!" Miss Joan retaliated.

"Get out!" Miss Marjorie cried. "Get out, get out!"

James and Mandy didn't know if she meant them or her sister. Everything was chaos. Mandy was growing sure of just one thing, though: This was no place for a tiny kitten.

She knew this once and for all when Miss Joan raised her rolled newspaper and began to chase Miss Marjorie from the hall into the study, a room at the front of the house. In a panic to stop them from injuring each other, Mandy and James hurried after.

Mandy stopped short. The room was lined from ceiling to floor with old books. But on the many tables scattered about the room were glass cases, dozens of them. Inside the dusty cases, perched, poised, and perfectly preserved, were . . . stuffed animals!

A heron stood on one leg, forever fishing. An otter bared his teeth at an invisible enemy. A wildcat stared warily out, as if he knew he was about to be made extinct. Mandy squealed. Both hands flew to her cheeks.

"Let's go!" James said. For once, he took the lead.

He grabbed her hand and made a run for it, back through the littered hall. They didn't turn to see if they were being followed. They just ran.

"Hey, you two!" Miss Marjorie called.

But they covered the distance to the gate in record time, ignoring the grinning gardener as they fled. Outside the gate they paused for breath. "Well?" James gasped.

"No good," Mandy said, almost in tears. The door was closed; the ivy still smothered the walls. The house seemed empty and grim. It would be another five years before anyone dared to disturb it.

"I agree." They were both too shocked to think straight.

It was only the routine of riding over to look after things in the Williamses' kitchen that saved them. They fed the kittens and rode back home to news from Mandy's mom.

Dr. Emily smiled across the treatment table, where she was giving Snap the terrier an anesthetic to make him sleep. "A Mrs. Parker Smythe called," she said. "She's interested in one of the kittens!"

Six

Mandy was up early the next day. She'd done her chores, been over to feed Walton, and was back before her mom had finished breakfast.

"I'll take you up to the Parker Smythes in the car, if you like," Dr. Emily offered. "The appointment is for nine-thirty." It was the only other phone call about the kittens since the Misses Spry disaster, so Mandy felt glad her mother was coming along to give moral support.

"It's way out of the village, up by the Beacon." Dr. Emily opened the passenger door of their big four-wheel drive. "Hop in," she said: "Do we have to pick up James?"

"No. He came over earlier to feed the kittens, but he has a soccer game today, and his mom told him to take Blackie on an extra long walk, so he can't come."

"Do the Hunters still have that cat of theirs?" Dr. Emily fastened her seat belt.

"Benji? Yes, of course. Why?"

"He's getting a bit old, that's all."

They took the high road out of Welford. Soon a steep hill loomed ahead of them. On top there was a stone pillar, visible for miles around: the Beacon.

"I guess James is still recovering from yesterday?" Dr. Emily said, her eyes set firmly on the road ahead.

Mandy nodded. "We both are." Mandy was brave, but even she was rattled by the Spry sisters. She knew she was the least squeamish person around; she'd watched operations on stomachs, intestines, legs, and hearts. But she shuddered at the thought of the poor stuffed creatures in the library at The Riddings, glass-eyed, covered in dust.

"You have to remember it was the fashion a hundred years ago. Most people have thrown those glass cases full of birds and animals away by now. But don't blame the twins too much. Poor things." Dr. Emily spoke quietly. She pushed a stray strand of hair behind her ear.

"Yes," Mandy agreed. "Animals look so much better alive and out in the wild, not stuffed inside some rotten case!"

"I meant the sisters!" Her mom glanced across at her. The hill was beginning to flatten out now. They could see the Beacon just ahead. "They don't mean anyone any harm."

"What, those two horrible old things? Nobody ever goes near them, and all they ever do is argue!"

"Exactly," Dr. Emily said softly.

And Mandy had to sit and think about that as they pulled up outside a high hawthorn hedge with double iron gates, electronically controlled. BEACON HOUSE was written in big gold letters. And NO PARKING. TRESPASSERS WILL BE PROSECUTED.

Dr. Emily put on the parking brake. "Anyway, this looks more normal." She spoke into a little security box on the gatepost, then the gates opened as if by magic.

Mandy turned and took in the long-distance view of the valley: its odd-shaped patchwork fields, scattered hillside farms, the road and river running parallel along the bottom, and Welford's two main streets crisscrossing in the far distance.

Then she turned again and followed her mother up the drive. They went on foot through a small patch of trees, up to the big white house.

"What's that?" Mandy whispered. She pointed to a flat paved area the size of a tennis court, but marked with large white circles. It wasn't a tennis court anyway, because *that* was on the other side, to the right of the house.

"Helicopter pad?" Dr. Emily suggested. She rang the doorbell.

Mandy gulped. A very blonde, very smartly dressed woman opened the door. She wore a white shirt and trousers, and gold necklaces, rings, bracelets. A lot of gold. Even her shoes had gold decorations sewn on.

Mandy felt her mother give her a little shove forward to speak. "Mrs. Parker Smythe?" she asked nervously.

The woman nodded. Her blonde hair stayed put. Not a highlighted strand moved. Her smile revealed two rows of perfectly even, perfectly white teeth between shiny pink lips. "Come in!" she said, like you heard it said in posh films, usually with "darling" on the end.

They went in, and she closed the door. "Come this way!" she said, all teeth and lipstick and gold things dangling. Through the white hall with Italian tiles and rugs, into the kitchen. "You must be Mandy? You put the nice pink sign in the village hall? I was picking up Imogen from the

Brownies and we saw your ad!" she gushed.

Mandy nodded. She was finding it hard to fit in a word. Anyway, the kitchen made her feel that being there in her jeans and T-shirt and talking out loud in her ordinary voice was a mistake. It wasn't a bit like the old pine table and quarry-tiled floor of her own kitchen. This kitchen had shiny blue glass bowls and white gadgets everywhere, and no food anywhere to be seen.

Mrs. Parker Smythe didn't seem to notice Mandy's shyness. "Imogen is my little girl. She's seven!" she said proudly, as if Imogen being seven was like winning the Olympic Games singlehanded.

"And this is Ronald, my husband. He's in satellite television!"

A balding man walked in, nodded, and walked out again. He wore the palest yellow V-neck sweater and tan checked trousers.

"He's going to play golf," Mrs. Parker Smythe told them. She shared another confidence: "With Jason Shaw! You know, Jason Shaw, the actor. They're very good friends, Ronald and Jason."

Mandy risked a glance at her mother but didn't dare ask, "Jason who?" Her mother was looking steadily out of the window, trying not to smile.

"We first met Jason when he came to film here, you know," Mrs. Parker Smythe rattled on. "For an episode of *The Swallows in Spring*, this time last year. They used our swimming pool!"

Mandy gulped again. She couldn't help it. Maybe tough little Smoky would be the right kitten for the Parker Smythes. The rough-and-tumble one. He'd bring them down to earth.

"Yes, our swimming pool was used as a set for the program. It belongs to the right period for the series. So Jason and the crew came up. That's how we met!" Mrs. Parker Smythe bubbled on. She seemed to have forgotten all about the reason for their visit.

"Did you want a kitten for your little girl?" Mandy managed to fit in at last. Mr. Parker Smythe wandered in and out again, apparently looking for something.

"Yes, well, we have so much space here." Mrs. Parker Smythe spread her arms and her jewelry jangled. "And such a big garden! And of course we have security cameras out there, so there's no danger of the poor little mite getting lost or anything."

Mandy noticed her mother's eyebrows shoot up a fraction of an inch.

"And when we're away at our house in Italy, we still have Mrs. Bates, our housekeeper, to come in and look after the kitten, feed it, and so on." Mrs. Parker Smythe looked at her gold watch. "Would you please excuse me a moment?" She dashed off after her husband.

"I wonder what he's lost?" Mandy whispered.

"His helicopter?" her mom said. But no; they heard huge blades begin to whir out on the pad. Clearly it had been wheeled out from its hangar and prepared for takeoff.

They grinned. Mandy felt more relaxed. "What if Smoky doesn't fit in here because he's only a plain, ordinary tomcat?"

"Let's meet the little girl first, before we make any decisions," Dr. Emily said.

Mandy nodded. She had to admit, once again, the signs were not all that promising.

"Oh, good, you're still here!" Mrs. Parker Smythe floated back in after a few minutes. "Now you must come and meet Imogen!"

She led them out of the kitchen across a giant sunroom full of artificial palms and pink-flowered cane furniture. But this was only a link to the house's main attraction, its indoor heated pool. This opened up from the sunroom through wide double doors.

The poolside was dazzling white and the water was deep blue. There was a fountain at one end, and windows from ceiling to floor all down one side. And there in the water, swimming like a walrus with just its nose and whiskers out of the water, was Imogen Parker Smythe.

"Imogen!" her mother called out, clapping her jeweled hands smartly.

Imogen ignored her.

"Imogen, we have visitors!" her mother called again.

No response. Imogen swam around and around the fountain at the deep end. Mandy was amazed by her rudeness. *I'd never get away with that!* she thought.

Mrs. Parker Smythe sighed. "Come along, we'd better go down." She went along the poolside carrying an apricot-colored bathrobe and a towel for her daughter. Mandy and Dr. Emily followed.

"Imogen!" Mrs. Parker Smythe said in a coaxing voice. She crouched beside the water. "Now come along, darling. Come and talk to Mommy about a sweetie, itsy-bitsy kittie for Immikins!"

Mandy swallowed hard. She stuck both hands into her jeans pockets. *Yuk!* she thought. She just hoped no one could read her mind.

"Won't!" Imogen retorted, swimming in smaller circles.

"Oh, come on, darling! Remember, we talked about a sweet little furry kitty for you just this morning at breakfast. Remember?"

"No!" Imogen spat out water like a whale.

"Immie!" Mrs. Parker Smythe was getting wet. "Now come along out of there immediately, or I'll call your daddy!"

With a great sigh and much splashing, Imogen Parker Smythe heaved herself out of the water. She was a mousy-haired, slightly overweight little girl with a constant scowl. She squirmed as her mother wrapped her in the bathrobe. She pushed away the towel offered for her dripping hair. Instead she shook her head from side to side like a dog.

"Hello," Mandy said. She forced herself to take the lead in this conversation.

Imogen tossed her head and sniffed up great drips of water.

"I hear you want a kitten?" Mandy went on.

Sniff. Sniff.

"I've got four kittens. Four tiny ones just a few days old. But soon their mother will finish feeding them, and after that they'll need really good names and somebody to look after them!" Mandy explained in what she thought was a clear, sensible way.

"I know that!" Imogen snorted. "Everyone knows that!"

"Immie!" Mrs. Parker Smythe chirped.

"They'll need good homes, and someone very kind and careful to look after them!" Mandy said in a much cooler voice.

"What color are they?" Imogen demanded, eye to eye with Mandy. "I want a white one!"

Mandy paused. "Well, the color isn't that important, really, is it? I mean, a kitten isn't a kind of toy, is it? It's a real live animal, you know. Soon it'll grow into a big cat that will still need to be fed and taken to the vet and somewhere clean and airy to sleep. In fact, it will need lots of looking after!"

Imogen turned to her mother. "I only want a white one!" she whined.

"But Immikins!" Mrs. Parker Smythe looked helplessly at Mandy.

"You said I could have a white one!" The child stamped her foot. "A white kitten! A fluffy white one with long fur! I want one! I want one!"

Mandy was furious. She felt like stepping right up to the revolting girl and pushing her back into the swimming pool. "Kittens are not toys!" she repeated. "And they don't have to match your color scheme!"

"Mandy!" Dr. Emily warned under her breath.

But Imogen was equal to the fight. She took a long look at Mandy, then she screwed her face tight and whined loudly. "O-o-ooh, Mommy, make the horrible, nasty girl go away! I don't like her! Make her go away, Mommy!"

Mrs. Parker Smythe fell for it. "There, there, Immikins, don't cry!" she said. She cuddled her daughter at a distance, so as to keep dry. "You don't have to have a kitty if you don't want one, darling. There, there!"

Mandy saw Imogen's face peep out at her from behind pudgy little fists. Imogen sneered up at her. "That got you!" she seemed to be saying.

Dr. Emily was pulling at Mandy's arm. "Time to go," she urged.

But Mrs. Parker Smythe had stopped cuddling Imogen and came toward them. "Pay no attention," she whispered. "Imogen's in one of her moods. You can bring the kitten anyway. I'll talk her into it."

But Mandy stood her ground. She was determined to have her say. "Mrs. Parker Smythe," she announced, "I'm afraid this would never work!"

Mrs. Parker Smythe's gold jewelry trembled as she went back and bent over her daughter.

Mandy continued. "To keep a pet you have to be a sensible, caring person. Animals have rights, you know, and one of those rights is to belong to a good, responsible owner!" She paused for breath, but there was no stopping her now. "And I'm afraid Imogen just doesn't qualify! I can't imagine anyone *less* suited to look after Smoky, Patch, Amy, or Eric!"

She glared down at them as they hugged each other by the side of their swanky pool. She turned on her heel. Her sneakers squeaked on the wet tiles all the way down to the French doors, but she didn't care. She swung through the sunroom, the designer kitchen, the hall. Dr. Emily caught up with her halfway down the driveway.

"Sorry, Mom, for being rude," Mandy said. But her mother didn't seem to mind as they marched out to the car, shoulder to shoulder.

"No good," Dr. Emily sighed and opened the door.

Mandy sank back in the passenger seat. She felt bitter about spoiled little rich kids and their soft mothers. And she was panicking about the kittens. Two replies to their ads so far, and two disastrous results! "No, no good again!" she said.

Tears of disappointment threatened to burst out, but she bit them back. She had to keep on looking. She had to succeed!

Seven

The weekend was almost over, and still the kittens were homeless. Mr. Williams would kick them out of his kitchen on Thursday or do something dreadful. For him, they weren't creatures with feelings. They were just nuisances to be gotten rid of.

"That's how some people think," Mandy's dad explained. "Especially some older people around here. You don't get sentimental about animals when you live on farms or in the villages. When Mr. Williams was young, they drowned unwanted kittens in the rain barrel behind the barn. I don't suppose they even thought it was cruel."

Mandy shuddered. As far as she was concerned, it was murder.

"Come on, help me take this young fellow over to Ernie's!" Dr. Adam suggested. He picked up the plastic cage containing the baby squirrel. "I've checked him over and he's as right as rain. He can go into the run at the back of Ernie's house and we'll see how he gets along."

They set off on foot down their lane to the main street. It was a sunny afternoon, with blossoms everywhere. Gardeners were out with their trowels and pruners, making the flowers stand at attention. "Good afternoon," people said pleasantly. Some stopped to look at the squirrel and pass the time of day.

Mandy liked the fact that everyone knew her father. He'd been born up at Lilac Cottage and had lived in Welford all his life, except for his college days in York. The older villagers still called him "young Adam" or "Tom Hope's lad." They knew he was a brainy boy, he'd been to college, and he was known as a decent vet. At any rate, he was one of them.

The women came out of their houses and made a fuss over Mandy, while the men described problems with moles on their lawns or a sheep stuck in the cattle fence at the back of the Janekis' farm.

The squirrel scampered in its cage, accepting offers of peanuts through the bars.

At last Mandy and her father reached the Fox and Goose. "It's only taken us an hour and fifteen minutes!" she remarked.

Dr. Adam laughed and went into the tavern for lemonade. They spent another fifteen minutes in the last rays of sunshine, sitting on a bench, gossiping.

"Right!" Dr. Adam wiped his beard and stood up. He sounded purposeful at last. "You bring the squirrel, Mandy."

She followed him across the cobble stone courtyard of the pub. The squirrel scuttled in its cage.

"That used to be the forge," Dr. Adam said. He pointed to the plush restaurant at the side of the pub.

"I know, Dad, you've told me!"

He carried on regardless. "My own grandfather had the place in the 1920s."

"I know, Dad!" Boy, was he embarrassing sometimes. Mandy shuffled from one foot to the other. Soon she'd have to ride over to Walton for the regular evening feeding. The kittens were doing well on the special liquid food, and Walton herself was looking sleeker. Mandy was pleased with their progress. "Come on, Dad, let's go!"

He turned and grinned. "Sorry, sweetie!" And he led the way again, down the side of the pub to a row of tiny two-story stone cottages that had seen better days. There were five cottages, all with broken-down doors, unruly ivy and great stone slabs making a path along the length of the row. Most of the front doors stood open in the sunshine.

"Now then, young Adam!" a gruff voice said.

Mandy and Dr. Adam stopped at the first house. She might have known they wouldn't make it to Ernie's without at least two more interruptions.

"Hello, Walter. Lovely day!" Dr. Adam stopped and leaned in at Walter Pickard's door. "How are things?"

"Mustn't grumble," the old man said. "Hello there, young miss!"

Mandy smiled hello. Walter never remembered the name of anyone under thirty. It was just "young miss" or "young sir." He was a retired butcher, a Wednesday evening church bell-ringer alongside her grandfather, and, what's more, a cat lover! Two lovely old ginger cats sunned themselves on his front doorstep.

"What have we here?" Walter said, bending and tapping the cage. Inside, the squirrel sat up and begged. "Hey, look at that!" Walter said, half laughing. He went off down the dark, narrow hallway and came back with a piece of cracker, which he fed to the squirrel.

Mandy liked Walter. He was a big man, but his deep voice was gentle, and his lined face under its flat cloth cap was always smiling. His wife had died last year, but Walter's three cats still kept him company. Mandy liked him because of his smile and his cats. What she couldn't understand was how he'd spent his entire working life in a butcher's shop. All those cold sides of beef hanging on their hooks. All those dead chickens. Mandy shuddered. She was glad she was mostly a vegetarian. These days she hardly ever ate meat.

Dr. Adam glanced at his watch. "Do you know if Ernie's in?" he asked.

Walter nodded. "Most likely."

"In that case I'll just get this little fellow over there." Dr. Adam picked up the cage, saw Mandy was busy stroking the ginger cats, and said, "You stay, Mandy, and tell Walter the story of Ernie Bell and the orphan squirrel!" Then he wandered off down the lane.

Mandy recounted the sad story of the squirrel.

"Ernie Bell!" Walter said, shaking his head. "He's adopting a squirrel, that miserable old devil!" It was like saying he, Walter Pickard, had won the soccer pools.

Mandy had her hand deep in the soft, warm fur of one of the old ginger cats when an idea struck her. She looked up from her cross-legged position on the path. "Walter, how many cats do you have?" she asked casually. But the excitement of the idea was beginning to make her heart beat faster.

"Three," he said. He sat down heavily on an old wooden stool just inside the doorway. "That one's called Scraps because she feeds on any scraps I give her. She's not the least bit fussy." He pointed to the one Mandy was stroking. "And that's Missie over there, because she's a proper little madam and only eats the best fish and chicken breast." This other ginger cat was contentedly purring in the sun. "Then there's Tom. He's indoors."

Mandy listened quietly, but she thought furiously.

"We used to have another one, you know," Walter went on. "My Mary loved cats, and it was her favorite, Susie, that passed away just after Christmas." He sat with his own memories for a while, then pulled himself together. "Susie was a dainty little cat, just like my Mary. That's why she was her favorite." He smiled. "Yes, indeed."

Mandy nodded. She knew it was now or never.

"Why not get another?" she said. "It just so happens I'm looking for homes for kittens right now, and there's one little dainty one, a little tortoiseshell called Amy, who'd be just right for you, I'm sure!"

Walter listened. He seemed to like the idea. "A tortoiseshell?"

"Yes. They're only a few days old, and we're partly having to hand-rear them, James Hunter and I, because the mother's too weak. She was a stray. But we'll need homes for all of them. Good homes!" She stressed the "good" and looked up at Walter.

He blew out his cheeks like a trumpeter. "A tortoiseshell?" he repeated. Mandy pictured a young kitten scampering about on the warm flagstones all summer long, jumping up at his wallflowers, tumbling in over the step.

"A really lovely little tortoiseshell!" she insisted. She held her breath.

"Aye, I'd love one," Walter sighed.

"Oh, it'd be a perfect home for Amy!" Mandy told him. "It's nice and quiet back here, off the road, and the older cats would look after her, and you know all about kittens. It would be ideal!"

Say yes, she prayed. *Say yes!*

But a shadow crept down the hallway. A big

bruiser of a shadow padding up to the doorstep in the sinister shape of Tom.

"Hello!" Mandy said to the barrel-shaped cat. He stood foursquare in his doorway. He bared his teeth and hissed. "Hello there!" She ran her fingers up and down the flagstones. "Come here!" she coaxed. He ignored her game. Sulkily he padded across the step, back and forth, strong shouldered, wide mouthed. He was a black-and-white bully with a pirate's black patch over his left eye, a chewed left ear, and ragged whiskers.

"Ah, Tom!" Walter said with a sigh of regret.

Tom arched his back at Mandy and spat. He padded around the two ginger females, just checking up on them. Then he stood and stared again at Mandy.

"There's Tom to consider, you see," Walter explained. "Scraps and Missie would be fine. But not Tom." The old man shook his head. "Just take one look at him. He'd eat a new kitten for breakfast!"

Mandy could believe it. Never had she seen a cat like Tom; a heavyweight, a bouncer, a sumo wrestler of a cat!

"No," Walter said sadly. "Much as I'd like to, I'm afraid old Tom wouldn't be happy with a stranger around the place. You can see my problem?"

Mandy nodded. Though she was desperate, she had to agree.

"Never mind, Thomas, no one's going to come upsetting you." Walter bent forward to scratch the chewed-up old ear. "Just relax, old man!"

The cat blinked and tilted its colossal head in victory. He'd staked out his territory and won.

Sadly, Mandy got to her feet. Such a missed opportunity! But her dad was returning with the empty cage. "Ready?" he asked.

They said their good-byes to Walter and set off

across the pub yard. The old man continued to sit on his stool, cats at his feet.

"You know," Dr. Adam said, glancing backward, "old Walter's fond of cats. Why don't you —"

"It's all right, Dad," Mandy interrupted, "I already have. I asked him, and he says he'd like another kitten, but Thomas the Terrible wouldn't appreciate it." She joked, but she was feeling very low. "In the end he said no."

"Ah, well," Dr. Adam said, swinging the empty cage, lost in his own thoughts.

All the gardeners had gone inside for tea, so their walk home was much quieter and quicker. Dr. Emily had prepared their own evening meal, knowing that Mandy would want to ride over to school before it got dark. No one mentioned the kittens. If they had, Mandy felt she might have broken down. And her mom and dad knew when not to make a fuss. She ate, then packed her bag. She met James at the post office and together they rode to Walton.

Mr. Williams was in a very bad mood.

"It's Sunday night," Mrs. Williams reminded them. "He always gets like this on a Sunday night."

He'd been stamping about the kitchen when they arrived, but as soon as he saw them, he grunted, took his Sunday newspaper, and headed out of the room.

"It's because it's Monday tomorrow," Mrs. Williams explained. "W-O-R-K! The dreaded four-letter word."

Then Tuesday, then Wednesday, Mandy thought with a lurch. She wanted to stop the clock or at least to stretch the days. The trouble was, as each visit to the kittens came and went, she grew fonder of them. They were about five inches long and weighed just three or four ounces or so. They hadn't yet struggled to their feet, and their eyes were still closed. Smoky was strongest, but Patch put up a good fight for food. Amy and Eric were patient, more content.

Now was the time to ask Mrs. Williams if they could gently tip the laundry basket onto its side so the kittens could begin to get a feeling of the outside world. "And then Walton might be ready to move them to a new nest," Mandy suggested.

"What, tip it over and leave it there?" Mrs. Williams asked. She looked doubtful. "It'd make the place look a terrible mess!" But in the end she agreed. The basket could be tipped onto its side.

As James and Mandy fed each of the kittens in turn, Mr. Williams stamped back in. He was wearing a very clean, very stiff white shirt and a maroon tie. He looked smart in his dark suit, but he walked awkwardly, Mandy noticed for the first time. He frowned at the turned-over laundry basket.

Mrs. Williams leaped to her feet. She was ready for the evening service at church, in her beige dress and silk scarf. "Now, Eric!" she warned. She saw him glaring at the two kittens who happened to be pulling by mistake at the sleeve of his best blue shirt. They were seeking out Walton, but getting tangled in the shirt instead. "It's only till Wednesday night!" she promised.

He didn't even grunt. He just stamped out onto the porch.

"Good thing it's Sunday!" Mrs. Williams whispered.

"Why?" James asked.

"Eric never swears on a Sunday," she said. She raised her eyebrows. "Otherwise the air in the kitchen would be blue as that shirt!" She sighed as she picked up her shiny brown handbag. She checked her keys. "Lock the door when you go," she reminded them. Then she followed her husband down the road to church.

Mandy shook her head. The kittens were all safe for the night. James was washing Walton's food bowl and saucer, and the mother cat was coming to Mandy for a final grateful stroke before she settled down with her kittens. "I wish . . ." Mandy said. But she never finished the sentence.

James felt helpless, too, as they checked the kitchen, turned off the light, and locked the door. "That's what I like about computers," he said out of the blue as they got on their bikes.

"Huh?" Mandy said. "What are you talking about?" James sometimes came out with these odd things.

"Computers. That's what I like about them. They're straightforward and simple, and they never make you feel bad."

"Not like people and animals, you mean?"

He nodded. "And you can just switch them on and off, no problem."

They rode along for a while in silence.

"But they break down!" Mandy objected. You shouldn't prefer machines to live things, she thought.

"So do animals," he said. Another silence. "Like Benji."

"Oh, what's wrong with Benji?" Mandy asked. James had had Benji for as long as she could remember; he was a beautiful, docile black tomcat.

"Dunno," James said. "My mom has to bring him into the Ark tomorrow morning to see if your mother can find out."

Mandy nodded and sighed. "Well, see you tomorrow, early?" she said by way of good-bye.

"Tomorrow early," James promised, as they each rode their separate ways.

Eight

One little victory would be enough, Mandy thought. One home for one kitten. It wasn't asking much, and it would be a start. She went through the names they had so far, just to make sure that none of them would do.

Thinking hard, she handed Simon a thermometer to take the temperature of a Border collie who was just recovering from parvovirus. It was only because she was so young and strong that she'd survived.

Simon stroked the dog's long, black coat. "At least they'll remember to have her vaccinated from now on," he said.

Mandy nodded, but she was thinking of Miss Marjorie Spry. Surely even she could remember to open a can of cat food each day. The kitten could be given a quiet, cozy corner in the garden shed if that old gardener would clear a space. Mandy stopped scooping meat into the dog bowls and stood, fork poised.

"A penny for them," Simon said with a smile. He was looking at his watch.

"What?" Mandy was imagining Amy snugly curled up behind the old flowerpots and garden shears.

"A penny for your thoughts!" Simon took the fork and went on preparing bowls of food for their resident cocker spaniel and two black Labradors. "You don't usually daydream on the job," he said.

"Oh, sorry!" Mandy gave a sigh. Of course, The Riddings was hopeless. Simon had broken her dream. She recalled the frozen snarl of the stuffed wildcat, the glass stare of the heron. All those dusty cases with dead animals in them. She was afraid it would never work to send Amy there, and the poor kitten was still homeless.

"Best get a move on," Simon said. "Here, you do the hamster dishes next, while I clean out the cages. And remember Flopsy and company out back!"

Mandy took the scoop full of rabbit food out into

the backyard. There was always the Parker Smythe mansion for Smoky, she told herself. She knew she was clutching at straws, though. How long would it be before the kitten lost its novelty there? Two days? Mandy sighed again. And that was only if Imogen would accept a gray cat. No, she wouldn't wish Imogen Parker Smythe on her worst enemy, let alone on precious Smoky.

If only Walter Pickard's old tomcat had been better tempered! Mandy stood there with a handful of oats and sunflower seed mixture, deep in thought.

When she went inside, Simon had finished the hamster cages. He took a last look at her and in his quiet way took charge. "Look," he said. "I'll finish here, so you can get off to school early again."

"What? Oh, yes, thanks!" Mandy dusted off her hands and scrambled out of her white coat. "Is that the time? I must run!"

She was out of Animal Ark and in her school uniform when she bumped into her mom on the stairs. "Any phone calls?" she asked, hoping for more responses to the signs.

"No," Dr. Emily said.

"Right." She hadn't really expected any this time. Her hopes were not high.

Then she was out of the house, up the lane on

her bike to meet James outside McFarlane's. Her mind was still working overtime. *I suppose I could always try Walter again*, she thought as she screeched to a halt. James was already there.

"Sorry I'm late!" she said.

James was quieter than usual as they rode to school, but Mandy had a lot on her mind, too.

School went by in a semidaze. She got two questions wrong in history and a lecture from Mr. Holmes. "What's wrong, Amanda? This isn't like you. Watching too much television, I expect. Now just pay attention, please!" Mandy's face felt red and hot, and she tried to concentrate.

She was thinking of the kittens when a group of friends asked her if she was going to the dance on Friday. Mandy didn't answer. "Oh, be like that!" one said. They were all giggling about something or other. "Don't think we care whether you come or not! You're not the center of the universe, Mandy Hope!" And they flounced off.

Mandy shrugged. It was time to go and feed the kittens.

And she was still thinking of them when James met her after school and told her quietly that he had to go straight home tonight. He'd promised his mom.

Mandy nodded. "See you tomorrow then," she

said. She had a plan in her head; not much of a plan, but she'd decided she would visit Walter again. She'd feed the kittens first, then she'd drop by the cottages. Anyway, it couldn't do any harm. She'd invent an excuse; maybe she'd visit Ernie Bell's squirrel and just "happen" to call on Walter. He mustn't think she was pestering on purpose.

"Hello, young miss!" Walter greeted her from his open door. "Where's that grandfather of yours gone? I haven't seen him around here lately."

Mandy propped her bike against the end wall. "Hi, Walter." She tried to sound casual. "He and Grandma are off on a camping trip in their new van." She gave him one of her cheeriest smiles. It was an effort, but she wanted to be bright and breezy.

"Camping!" Walter said with a low whistle. "At their age!"

"Not exactly." She explained the luxuries of the modern mobile home. "It has a fridge, electricity, everything!"

"Hmph! Don't they have a fridge and electricity at their house?"

"Yes."

"Well, then, what's the point?" Walter said. His ginger cats came padding elegantly down the hall.

Mandy gave in and changed the subject. She stroked Scraps and Missie. "I just popped over to see Mr. Bell's squirrel," she said casually. "To see if he's settled in okay."

Walter nodded. "Yes, if he'll see you," he said. "Ernie doesn't always answer his door!"

"I'll be back in a minute," she said.

She walked up the flagstone path to the end of the row. She knocked hard. The green door was faded and flaking; it needed a good coat of paint. And it had an old lion knocker that hadn't been cleaned for years. It was stiff with disuse. She knocked again.

"Hold your horses, hold your horses!" Ernie grumbled from inside. She heard bolts sliding, locks turning. Finally Ernie opened his front door.

Mandy heard Walter mumble and turn back inside his own house. She was left to face Ernie alone.

"Yes?" Ernie snapped. He was a small man with a shock of white hair rising back from his lined forehead. There was something birdlike about his sharp nose, his bright, dark eyes. He wore an old vest and a shirt without a collar. "Yes?" he said again, peering at Mandy.

She introduced herself as the vet's daughter. "My

dad brought the squirrel yesterday. How is he?" she asked.

Ernie frowned. "Fine, fine. What do you want now? You can't have him back, you know. I've paid the bill!"

"No, I don't want to take him back," Mandy tried to explain.

"Good. It cost me a fortune just to have him checked over, I can tell you. But I paid!" he insisted. He stood there, frowning.

"No, I —" Mandy hesitated, then changed tactics. "What's his name?" she asked.

Ernie paused. "Sammy," he said, as if he didn't want anyone to hear. "All right?"

"Yes, it's a nice name. I was just wondering, could I take a look at him, please?"

She waited until Ernie made up his mind. He stared at her, thought a while, then nodded. "This way," he said at last.

He led her down a dark hallway, through his kitchen, and out into the backyard. Four cottages away, Walter was out in his garden. He leaned his forearms against his fence top. "Hello there, Ernie!" he greeted his unfriendly neighbor.

Ernie grunted. He stood by, watching suspiciously as Mandy inspected the squirrel run.

"Sammy!" Mandy called gently. There was a sturdy hutch at the far end of the run, with a small hole for an entrance, which only something as tiny and agile as a squirrel could use. The little creature poked out its round gray head.

"Here," Ernie said. "Tempt him with these!" He handed Mandy a few peanuts from his trouser pocket.

And Sammy bounded out of the hutch. He clung upside-down to the netting, swinging like a trapeze artist toward her. His feet never touched the ground.

Mandy held out the nuts in the palm of her hand. Delicately Sammy watched, reached out a paw, and snatched the food. He swung away to a safe distance, then nibbled.

Mandy studied him. This was only the second time she'd been this close to a squirrel. The run was ten yards long, made of timber and fine mesh. Very safe. "This is great!" she told Ernie, tapping the framework.

"Hmm." Ernie nodded. "It should be." He, too, was watching the squirrel, and his face had lost its frown. "I've had a fair bit of practice, you know. I was a carpenter for more than fifty years!" Then, as if he'd given away top secret information, his mouth clamped shut, and the frown returned.

"Well, it's great," Mandy said. "Really sturdy and safe. I'm glad Sammy's found such a good home!" It was almost enough to take her mind off homeless kittens. But she could see Walter over in his own yard, and she was desperate to talk with him. She remembered her real purpose: to persuade Walter and old Tom to change their minds. "Can I come and visit Sammy again?" she asked Ernie.

He swallowed hard, but he nodded slowly. "You can come again," he agreed. "It might not always suit me to answer the door, you understand. But you can always try."

He followed her out to the front of the house. "Well, Mr. Bell —" Mandy was about to turn and thank him again for showing her the squirrel, but the shabby green door was already closed. And like a figure in a Swiss cuckoo clock, Walter was already out at his own front door. As usual, he was not minding his own business.

Mandy wandered toward him. She was going to ask, "How's old Tom today?" and then gently add that perhaps Tom would take to a new kitten, if they introduced him to the idea gradually.

But Walter must have been a mind reader. She never got any further than "How's old Tom?" before he cut her short.

"It's no good you wheedling away, young miss!" Walter laughed at her surprise. "I know what you're going to ask, and Tom's answer is still no!"

As if to confirm this, Tom came barreling around the corner at top speed and rammed right into Mandy's bike. Down it crashed. Tom wailed loudly, leaped over the spinning wheels, and vanished across the pub yard.

"See?" Walter said, laughing again. He picked up the bike. "Nothing's safe with our Tom on the scene!" He turned to Mandy, then he looked down the row to Ernie's end house. "But you know something, I think we've just had an idea!"

"We have?" To Mandy it didn't feel as if anything was going right.

"Yes. You hit it off with old Ernie, didn't you?" Walter scratched his head, a sure sign that he was thinking.

"I suppose so," Mandy said doubtfully. "Listen, you don't think I should ask him?" Her eyes lit up. "I mean, you mean I should ask him to take a kitten?" She felt the idea light up all the dark corners of her mind.

But Walter was shaking his head. "No, no, I don't think you should ask him exactly."

Mandy's face fell again. "Why not? He likes animals. He rescued little Sammy, didn't he?"

"Yes, but Ernie would say no if you asked him directly. On principle, he always says no. He's a grumpy, cantankerous old so-and-so — that's Ernie."

Mandy had to agree. "So what's our idea?" she asked.

"It's this!" Walter got into a huddle with Mandy around the corner, out of sight.

The idea involved taking a very big risk. But then Mandy had forty-eight hours to solve four very big problems. She listened to Walter, she nodded, she considered it. She thought of Sammy snug in his custom-built hutch. She decided to risk it.

So she called home and said she'd be late. Then she rode back over to Walton.

Mrs. Williams watched with concern as Mandy gave Amy a special feeding and tucked her into a specially lined cardboard box. Amy peered up, unseeing, sniffed, then settled down. Walton came over, glanced in, looked up at Mandy, then retreated to the laundry basket. She sat quietly inside with her other three kittens, looking out.

"She trusts you!" Mrs. Williams said. "Poor lamb, she trusts you with her babies!"

Mandy nodded. It was a hard thing to do, to take

the kitten from her mother, but it was a hard thing Mr. Williams was threatening to do, and Walter's plan made it necessary. "Good girl, Walton," she said. Carefully she folded down the flaps of the cardboard box.

"I hope you know what you're doing!" Mrs. Williams whispered.

Mandy looked her in the face. Her heart was in her mouth as she nodded and went outside. She strapped the box onto her bike, nodded again at Mrs. Williams, tried not to think about Walton and the three kittens cozy in their basket, and set off across the field.

It was the most heart-stopping bike ride she'd ever made. Every bend, every hill she took at a snail's pace. She came down into Welford holding her breath. She stopped at the pub, out of sight of Walter and Ernie's row of cottages. Then she unstrapped the box and crept with it in through Walter's open door.

"Got it?" Walter asked.

Mandy nodded. She opened the box. Amy mewed at the light. "Are you sure this will work?" she asked again.

Walter's head went to one side. "Not sure," he said. "Not one hundred percent." He gazed down at tiny, helpless Amy. "She's just a skinny little thing!" He tickled her head.

"Ernie's got a mind of his own. You can bet he'll do exactly the opposite of what you ask. Always has. You say to him, 'Ernie, do me a favor, fix the latch on this back gate for me,' and he'll say straight back, 'What do you think I am, the handyman around here?' and he'll stamp off in the other direction. But if he thinks it's his idea and he sees your gate's broken, he'll make a point of coming up and he'll say, 'I saw your latch was broken, Walter, so I just got out my toolbox and fixed it for you.' Just like that!"

Mandy understood. "Like rescuing Sammy, you mean? It had to be his idea." She lifted Amy out of her box. "So if he finds a tiny kitten abandoned on his doorstep, he'll take her in?"

Walter nodded. "As long as he does think it's his idea! Then he'll want to keep her and look after her, just like the squirrel. He'll come along to me for advice because he knows I've got the three cats, and I'll suggest, very cunning, how much better it'd be to find a feeding mother until the kitten's properly on its feet. That's where you come in, little miss!"

Mandy looked hard at Amy. "Are you sure?"

He nodded again. "Ernie's got a heart of gold underneath it all!" Walter smiled. "Go on, young miss, what have you got to lose? That kitten will have a foster home and be back with her mother before you can say Jack Robinson!"

So Mandy took the precious bundle down the path. Amy squirmed in her hands, mewing piteously. "Shh!" she whispered. Could she do it? Mandy felt as if her heart would stop. Could she leave the poor little thing on a cold doorstep?

She almost stopped to retrace her steps. But what was the alternative? She had less than two days left. Forcing herself to go on, she stooped down by Ernie's front doorstep. She closed her eyes, backed away, and fled back to Walter's house.

"Now we just have to wait," Walter said. They stood inside his doorway, listening to Amy's tiny wail.

"Oh, quick!" Mandy breathed. "Please hear her and come quickly!"

But Ernie's door stayed shut.

Amy mewed her high-pitched sound. Would he hear it? They waited. Mandy leaned forward, desperately wanting to see if Amy was all right. But Walter pulled her back. "You mustn't let him see you!" he warned.

The wait seemed endless. Minutes went by. Amy's tiny howling continued.

Then finally they heard the metal bolts of Ernie's door. They heard the latch turn. The door scraped open. "What the — !" Ernie said. He grunted as he stooped. "Oh-aagh!" They heard him sigh as he picked up the kitten and straightened his old back. He stepped out onto the path. He took time to look up and down. He even carried Amy a few steps toward Walter's house, then he turned and went indoors, carrying the kitten.

"Well?" Mandy was still holding her breath. She looked at Walter.

Walter listened. He considered carefully. Then he brought up one hand in a thumbs-up sign. "I reckon it's worked!" he said.

They had to wait half an hour, maybe more, drinking tea and eating cookies, before they heard Ernie shuffling down the path to Walter's door.

"Say nothing!" Walter warned. "And stay here!" Mandy nodded.

"Now then, Walter," Ernie said. He poked his head inside the front door. "You know about cats!"

"I do, Ernie," Walter said. "I know something about them, at any rate." Mandy sat out of sight in the kitchen as Walter went down the hall to greet Ernie. "Why, what have you got there?" He managed to sound genuinely surprised.

"Kitten," Ernie said. "What's it look like?" He had wrapped Amy in an old gray sweater. "It's shivering." He showed the little bundle to Walter.

"Yes, it would," Walter said. "It's only a littl'un."

"It just turned up out of the blue," Ernie said. "I was just washing up when I heard it making a racket on my doorstep! I reckon its mother dropped it there; one too many to look after in the litter."

"Well, it must be your week for it," Walter said, keeping his voice flat this time. "First the squirrel, now this."

"I dunno about that. It just turned up." Ernie

stood there looking helpless. Peeping, Mandy could see the two old men head to head against the square of light in the doorway.

"Ah, well, I reckon you'll have to get rid of this one," Walter said. "Two orphans to look after is more than you can manage."

Mandy gasped and bit her lip. How could he? How could Walter take such a risk?

But Ernie gave Walter his eagle stare. "What do you mean, more than I can manage?" He wrapped Amy up carefully. "I've no intention of getting rid of it, Walter Pickard! No, this little kitten is here to stay!"

Mandy cried. She cried tears of silent joy.

"Aye, but how will you feed it? Look at it, poor little scrap. It needs feeding already," Walter insisted.

Ernie thought about this for a while. "That's why I'm coming to you, Walter. You know about cats."

Now it was Walter's turn to stand there looking awkward and sullen. "It's too young for me to handle. It needs a mother cat," he said. "One that's still feeding her own youngsters."

Ernie squared his shoulders and asked how they would set about finding such a thing; a mother cat that would feed his kitten until it was weaned? He'd like Walter to call the vet right then and there, on his telephone, and get the vet's young girl over there as quick as possible. "I reckon she'll know of just such a cat," Ernie said, hugging Amy to his chest.

"Oh, she'll know," Walter confirmed, giving a little smile.

Back in the kitchen, Mandy grinned. Walter's plan had worked perfectly!

"Then you go ahead and give her a call. You tell her I want her down at my cottage in fifteen minutes sharp!" Ernie instructed. "And tell her to bring something to carry a tiny kitten in. We need a mother cat right away, or my little kitten will starve to death!"

"Right!" Walter agreed.

"Right!" And Ernie marched on back home with Amy.

Walter came back grinning all over his face. Mandy sat on the kitchen stool and smiled through her tears. They'd found a home for Amy. At last they'd found one good home!

Nine

Mandy paid a visit to Ernie's, complete with her lined cardboard box. She fed Amy quickly and expertly, mixing the powdered food in a miniature feeding bottle. She held Amy in one hand, then stroked her abdomen with a forefinger to help her digest the food and get rid of the waste. Ernie didn't bat an eyelid at that.

"You have to do it, otherwise they hang on to it and get constipated," Mandy explained. "That's why the mother cats lick them."

"And how often will this mother cat have to feed it?"

"*She* needs feeding every couple of hours. And the mother will keep her warm, too," Mandy said.

Ernie picked up his kitten and said an awkward good-bye. His fingers looked broad and clumsy against Amy's tiny head, but he held her calmly. He gave her every scrap of his attention. He bent his white head, making encouraging little chucking noises with his tongue. Then he looked up. "I'll call her Twinkie!" he said.

Mandy started to protest, then bit her tongue hard. She couldn't tell Ernie that Amy already had a name. She swallowed and nodded. "Good idea." She took the kitten from Ernie and put her carefully in the box. "She'll be ready to come home in six or seven weeks," she promised.

So Amy became Twinkie. "Brilliant name, isn't it?" She greeted James with the news when they met in the village early next morning. But Mandy was so thrilled that the name hardly mattered. "Three more to go!" she said, full of new enthusiasm for the task. The morning was sunny. Things had begun to go right.

James nodded. He was looking pale and tired.

"What's wrong?" Mandy asked. She was peering in through the post office window to make sure that their sign was still up there on the bulletin board.

"Nothing." James shook his head and started to set off for school. He refused to look Mandy in the face as he mumbled, "Let's go."

"No, there is something wrong!" Mandy insisted. James was always shy and only got visibly excited about soccer. But today there was something making him even quieter than usual. He hadn't really reacted to the news about Amy. He hadn't said, "Great. Well done. I knew you could do it, Mandy!"

James shook his head again. He was staring down at his sneakers.

Mandy put one hand on the handlebar of his bike. "It's Benji, isn't it?" she said softly.

And James nodded.

"Oh, James, what's wrong with him?" She could have kicked herself. She'd been so full of her own news that she'd forgotten all about poor Benji being ill.

But James couldn't speak. He just sighed.

"He's going to be all right, isn't he? I mean, they'll fix him up at the Ark. It isn't anything serious, is it? What did my mom and dad say?" Mandy was beginning to sense something really awful. She'd never seen James look so sad.

And finally he came out with it. "Benji's dead," he said. "We had to have him put to sleep."

Mandy gasped. She expected the whole sky to come crashing down. Benji was dead. "Why?" She couldn't believe it.

The story came pouring out now. "He had some kind of tumor on his brain. We didn't know it was anything serious, only over the weekend he was a little groggy. No appetite, either." James paused to take a deep breath. "He kept staggering. My dad laughed and said he must have been out on Saturday night drinking. He looked pretty sorry for himself, so my mom said we'd take him into the Ark." He paused again and glanced at Mandy. "I think my mom knew," he said.

She nodded. "Then what?" No more Benji, she was thinking. No more Benji curled up on a seat in the Hunters' sunroom. No more Benji leaping from the sloping roof up through the bathroom window. Benji had always been there. He was part of the Hunter family.

James shrugged. He stared hard at his feet again. He was standing astride his bike, head down, miserable. "My mom took him in yesterday. By that time he could hardly stand. It was your mom who looked at him." Mandy realized that nothing in James's life had ever been so difficult for him to say. "Anyway, she said he had this growth on his brain. And there was nothing to be done in this kind of case."

"So?"

He sniffed. "So your mom explained that he'd be in a lot of pain."

"And *your* mom agreed to have him put to sleep?"

James nodded. "It would have been cruel to let him live."

For a second Mandy's hand touched James's. "That's true," she said.

Then there was a big silence. They both thought of Benji. Patient old Benji who'd grown up with them, who'd always let you pick him up any old way, and who always sat on your lap and let you tickle his chin. He'd put up over the years with all their rough treatment, and he'd never put in a cross word. He was a great cat.

"Let's go," James said. He glanced around at Mandy. "I told my mom to ask your parents not to say anything to you about it. I wanted to tell you myself."

Mandy nodded and followed on. Life, like the road over to Walton, was full of ups and downs.

It must have been hard for James, she thought, to help with the kittens this morning. He did the jobs as usual, before school and during lunch break. He listened as Mandy told Mrs. Williams how Amy, alias Twinkie, was safely back with Walton. And her future was secure.

"I hope this Ernie Bell person knows what he's doing with this kitten!" Mrs. Williams said primly. "I mean, men! They don't know how to look after things properly. They're not made that way!"

Mandy raised her eyebrows and glanced at James. He was busy with Smoky's feeding. "Oh, I don't know about that," she said.

"Not my Eric, at least," Mrs. Williams blundered on. "He's a bit old-fashioned in that respect."

As if on cue, Mr. Williams tramped in for his lunch. He ate in silence, glancing sullenly at the kitten activity in the far corner of the kitchen. "Tomorrow's D-Day!" he reminded them as he reached for his cap. "And don't you forget!"

D-Day. Death Day. Destruction Day. Deadline Day. Mandy didn't think it was possible to hate someone as much as she hated Mr. Williams just then. He stamped off down the garden path, tweaking a rose bush, perking up a primula.

"He's got to go see the headmaster!" Mrs. Williams whispered to Mandy. "He's been summoned!"

Mandy raised her head. She couldn't help that,

she thought. And all she really cared about right now was the kitten problem.

"Do you want to go right home after school?" she asked James, on their way into afternoon classes. She thought there was only so much she could ask him to do, considering Benji.

James looked up at the school shield in the entrance hall. Underneath there was a list of names of men who'd died in two wars, and underneath that was the school motto: "Through Suffering We Succeed."

"No," he said to Mandy. "I'll be there as usual."

James must have been thinking about poor Benji all through his game that afternoon. Mandy had glanced out of the science lab window down onto the soccer field, and she'd spotted him hanging about miserably on the goal line, most unlike him.

But when they met up after school, his face looked composed, even calm. "I just want to call my mom," he told her. "I'll be there in a minute."

So Mandy went on ahead. As usual, the routine of caring for the kittens took over, and she managed to push away the worry about James. She watched with delight their fluffy, wriggling little bodies, their ears beginning to unfold and perk up into position, their bruising battle to feed and to survive.

James came in just as she lifted Eric out of the basket for his feeding. She handed the kitten to him. "Here, you feed Eric," she said.

They worked in silence for a few minutes. Then James pushed his glasses up the bridge of his nose, sat back, and made an announcement. "I'd like Eric!" He said it quite straightforwardly, just like, "I'd like a candy bar!" or, "Tea with milk but no sugar, please!"

Mandy stared. "What did you say?"

"I'd like Eric," he repeated. "I've thought about it, and I'd like to adopt Eric!"

"Are you sure?" Mandy put Smoky back into the basket. "I mean, you're sure it's not too soon after . . . I mean, well, are you *sure*?"

"Yes. I called my mom. She agrees. If we're going to get another cat after Benji, we should do it right away." He looked down, half sad, half happy at the new scrap of life on his lap. "And I'm sure Benji wouldn't mind!"

Mandy waltzed around the kitchen. "Oh, great!" she said. "You hear that, Walton? Oh, wonderful! Oh, James!" She smiled and smiled.

Walton mewed.

There were practical things to arrange. When Mr. Williams threw the kittens out the next day, should James take Eric home then, or could they work out a way to keep Walton and the kittens together until they were weaned? A halfway house. That was the thing to work on, Mandy told James. She looked at Mrs. Williams, who was hovering in the doorway with her shopping basket.

"Don't ask me!" she muttered darkly. "Eric is in with the headmaster this very minute. Lord knows what's going to happen to any of us!" She went out tight-lipped, shaking her head.

"It's something we can work on," Mandy told James as they went out to their bicycles. "A halfway house. Anyway, we have two good homes. Two wonderful homes!" Mandy could have sung for joy as they rode home.

"Two to go!" Mandy told her mom as she flung her backpack in the corner of the hallway. She told her about James's decision to take Eric. "He's probably the grumpiest kitten of them all, like the person he's named after," she joked. "But James seems to like him!"

Dr. Emily smiled. "He's a good boy." Then she asked Mandy to help in the kitchen. "Your dad's out on an emergency call. One of Mrs. Janeki's sheep. But your grandfather called while you were out, just to let us know they're back."

Mandy nodded. "Did they have a good time?"

"He didn't say. But he said your grandma had gotten a reply from the prime minister." Dr. Emily looked puzzled. "Could that be right?"

"Yes. But that was quick." Mandy asked if she could run up to see them.

"After supper," Dr. Emily said. She always had to remind her daughter to slow down enough to eat. "What's the point of me preparing all these vegetarian meals for you if you won't even sit down and eat one!" she complained.

Mandy gave her a hug. "Okay, Mom, after supper!"

The camper sat in the driveway, splashed but splendid. "Hi, Grandma! Hi, Grandpa!" Mandy burst in on them. She reported the good news about Twinkie ("What a name!") and Eric. She said James was a hero, a real hero!

"Oho!" her grandfather raised his eyebrows.

"No, Grandpa, not like that!" she said.

"That's what they always say. I think Mandy's got a soft spot for young James."

"Stop teasing, Thomas!" Mandy's grandmother warned. "Anyway, she's come to see my letter from the prime minister, haven't you, honey!"

Mandy nodded and laughed. "Sorry, Grandma. It's just that the kittens have been taking up all my time. Did you have a good vacation?" she remembered to ask.

There was a small silence. "Yes," Grandma said. "But about this letter from 10 Downing Street. See, official notepaper!" She waved the reply in Mandy's face.

"'Yes' means 'Yes, but,'" Grandpa put in. "And then we quickly change the subject!"

"Why, what happened? Did the camper break down?"

"Break down!" he exclaimed. "You must be joking!"

"Of course not," Grandma said. "The camper was perfect. But Scarborough wasn't."

"Not sunny?"

"Sodden," Grandma conceded. "Forty-two hours of solid rain. We counted!"

"Ah," Mandy said. "What a shame."

"Yes, but this letter here, see!" Grandma waved it before starting to read:

"Dear Mrs. Hope:

The Prime Minister acknowledges receipt of your letter. While he recognizes your concern about the continued existence of your local sub post office, he wishes me to point out that government policy on the issue is the concern of one of his junior ministers.

Accordingly he has asked me to pass on this matter to the relevant department.

Yours sincerely,
E. B. Whyte
(Assistant private secretary to
the Prime Minister)"

"There!" Mrs. Hope flung the cream-colored letter onto the table.

"What does it mean?" Mandy asked. "Are they going to close the post office or not?"

"It doesn't mean yes, it doesn't mean no. It doesn't mean anything!" Grandma said indignantly.

"It means they've passed the buck," Grandpa said. "As usual."

"They won't get away with it!" Grandma insisted.

Grandpa muttered in a stage whisper, "Watch it, Mandy, she's on the warpath!"

Grandma ignored him. "We'll have a campaign. Save our post office!" She stood up and strode across the room.

Mandy was enjoying this, her grandmother on her high horse.

"I'll have to organize everything, of course!" There was a glint in Grandma's eye.

Bells began to ring in Mandy's head. In fact, they set up a giant racket! Did this mean her grandparents would have to put their feet firmly back on Welford ground?

"This'll take a lot of time and energy, Grandma," she pointed out.

"Who cares?" Grandma swept around the room. "It's important! In fact, it's vital! We'll design a logo for our campaign. A heart shape, to show our post office is at the heart of the village!" Her hair was coming loose from its comb, and she was looking very fiery.

"I'm glad I'm not the poor little prime minister!" Grandpa laughed.

"Does this mean you might not go to Portugal?" Mandy asked. "I mean, you might have to stay at home more to run this campaign."

Grandma stopped in her paces. Grandpa said, "Ha!"

"We-ell," Grandma said. "We might not go quite so far afield as we thought." She gave Mandy a little grin. "The fact is, we missed you all terribly; you and your mom and dad, and this old place!" She sighed. "We're a pair of old softies, after all!"

"And then there's my tomatoes to consider," Grandpa said thoughtfully. "I'll have to talk nicely to my tomatoes!"

Mandy looked at them, bursting to ask the question. She took a great, deep breath. "Does this mean you might be willing to take a kitten after all?"

They broke into smiles, both of them. They hugged her. "We thought you'd never ask!" They looked at each other. Clearly they'd been thinking about it all the time they'd been away in soggy Scarborough.

"Smoky!" Mandy said, breathless.

"On two conditions," Grandma added.

"What?" She glowed with happiness. A home for the third kitten. A home just up the hill from Animal Ark. Mandy couldn't believe it.

"First, you've got to agree to come up and feed him whenever we do go away for a couple of days," Grandma said. "When we go off in the camper to lovely Wales, or wherever."

This was hardly a condition! Mandy nodded, speechless. She'd love to feed Smoky. Then he'd be half hers, wouldn't he? She just sat there nodding.

"Second!" Grandpa said, frowning and trying to look serious. "You must swear to water my tomatoes!"

"Oh, yes," she said. She'd even talk to them. "Oh, yes, yes!"

Ten

Thursday came, and Mandy woke three quarters happy, one quarter sad. Her heart felt pulled apart over Patch; poor little Patch, the only kitten still left homeless.

Dr. Emily looked at her across the breakfast table. "Problem?" she asked.

"You realize what day it is," Mandy said miserably.

"Thursday," her father said helpfully over the top of his newspaper.

"Yes, Thursday. And I've found homes for three of the kittens, but there's still one left over! Today's the deadline!" The word "deadline" had an awful hollow ring.

"Hasn't the mother cat decided to move off to a new nest site yet?" Dr. Adam asked.

Mandy shook her head. "No, she's still there in the kitchen, in the laundry basket. And today's the day *he* throws them out!"

"You mean Mr. Williams," Dr. Emily corrected her. "Not 'he.' So what next?"

"Grandma and Grandpa say they don't mind if the kittens and Walton move in with them until the kittens are weaned in about six weeks." Mandy managed a smile of relief. It had been a close call all around.

"But?" her mother asked.

"But they say the same thing as you. They say I have to find a home for Patch. Otherwise it's cruel to keep him alive!" Her eyes filled. "Poor Patch!"

"It's true. You can't just turn him out to fend for himself when the time comes. He has to have a home!" Even her softhearted father was telling her the same thing; the thing she didn't want to hear.

"Dad!" she cried.

"There's no 'Dad!' about it," her mother said firmly. "Look, Mandy, you've done brilliantly to find these three homes. We think you're wonderful!"

"Don't!" The tears brimmed over and down her cheeks.

Dr. Emily looked across at Dr. Adam. Mandy thought she spied a glimmer of hope through her tears. "Listen, sweetie, I'll come over and see you at school this lunchtime, all right?"

"What for?" Mandy said, sniffing and drying her eyes.

"Wait and see. I can't promise anything yet." Dr. Emily smiled and patted Mandy's hand. "Just wait and see."

That lunchtime Mandy fed Patch with an aching heart. James was busy with little Eric, and the other two kittens were already snuggled down in the basket, when there was a knock at the door.

"Hello. Is Mandy here?" a voice said to Mrs. Williams.

She recognized her mom, but the misery of looking down at Patch's little face, his eyes nearly open now, was too much. She couldn't bear to think about what might have to happen to him.

"Mandy?" her mom's voice repeated.

She looked up.

"I've brought someone with me." Dr. Emily was gentle but firm, as always. "Come in, and let's have a look at this little fellow."

Mandy felt suddenly surrounded by people and dragged back to the present from fears of the future. She pulled herself together. "Sorry," she said, standing up with Patch cupped in her hands. Her eyes focused on the visitors: Miss Marjorie and Miss Joan Spry!

What on earth was her mother up to? Mandy stood, ready to protest, but her mom gave her a meaningful look.

"This is the kitten Mandy came to see you about," Dr. Emily explained calmly. "And I'm sure she apologizes for running off so rudely." She smiled encouragingly at Mandy, who turned red and nodded without saying anything.

The two sisters nodded back and peered down at Patch. They poked their thin faces toward him curiously. They looked silently at each other.

Mandy had gotten over her shock. She trusted her mom to know what she was doing. And today the Spry twins didn't look so strange. Their untidy hair was combed back underneath straw hats, and their pastel summer coats made them look like quaint wedding guests.

"This is the only kitten left without a home," Mandy said. She offered Patch to one of the twins, not knowing which one.

The twin shook her head. "No, give him to Joan. See if she likes him," Miss Marjorie said. "She did promise to try to like him!"

Mandy held out the kitten again. With shaking hands Miss Joan took the little fur scrap and cradled him. She brought her face close to the kitten's and felt him lick her finger. "What is his name?" she breathed.

"Patch," Mandy said, holding her own breath. "He's just one week old!"

Joan looked up at her sister. The silence held them all like a net. Would she say yes? Would she give Patch a home and a future?

"Yes," she said at last. "I think I like him!"

"Of course you do! What did I tell you!" Miss Marjorie said.

And they all smiled and congratulated one another. They listened to Mandy's instructions about how a kitten should be treated: "Don't poke him, don't press him too hard, don't disturb him too much!" She said they should put him back with his mother now. "The excitement's too much for him," she said as she returned a squeaking Patch to his warm, dark nest.

The Spry twins smiled and thanked Mandy and went happily down the porch steps, arm in arm.

"See!" Dr. Emily said, head to one side. "Didn't I say they were harmless? You have to learn that all people are different, but that doesn't make them wrong. This kitten will be the best thing that's happened to the twins in an awfully long time!"

Mandy laughed and hugged her mom. "Oh, thanks!" she said. A great weight had lifted off her chest. She sighed and looked in on the kittens. They were curled up, snug and warm against Walton's sleeping body. "Four homes! We did it!"

"You did it," her mother said. "You and James!"

They looked at each other with huge grins on their faces. James turned red, even before Mandy hugged him.

When Miss Marjorie came back in for a moment, James stepped aside. Dainty as a canary in her pale yellow coat, Miss Marjorie headed straight for Mandy. "Thank you, my dear!" she said, patting her hand. "Thank you for bringing life back into our dark, dreary house. It's all due to you!" She beamed, nodded to James. "I'd best get back to my sister. We'll wait for you in the car," she told Dr. Emily before walking off again.

"Happy now?" Mandy's mom asked.

Mandy's eyes shone with tears again. She nodded, and they nearly spilled over. This time Mandy could say nothing at all!

* * *

School was coming to an end, and the great move began. "It's time for a new nest, Walton," Mandy told her gently. "And you don't even have to do it yourself, you lucky cat!"

"You're sure it'll be all right now?" Mrs. Williams fussed. There was no sign of her husband. It was a hot, humid day, threatening rain when Mandy's grandparents' camper pulled up in the playground. "Walton won't desert these kittens now?" She stood at the kitchen sink, grasping a dish towel.

"No, it'll work out okay, Mrs. Williams. Don't worry!" Mandy looked up and realized the old lady would miss Walton and the kittens after all. She smiled. "Honestly, Walton would fight to the death for them now. She's made a good strong bond with them. Thanks to you, of course!"

"Oh!" Mrs. Williams raised her hands and smiled modestly as Mandy's grandfather joined them in the kitchen.

"Yes, you gave them a good start," Mandy went on. "Now my grandmother and grandfather will keep a close eye on them up at Lilac Cottage!"

"Then what?" Mrs. Williams folded her dish towel into a precise rectangle. She laid it down on the drain board and smoothed it carefully.

"Then James will take Eric and give him a home," Mandy said, handing the kitten to him.

"And me and my wife will keep this little fellow," Grandpa said, lifting Smoky in one hand.

"Ernie Bell is waiting to have Amy — er — Twinkie. And now Patch has found a home at The Riddings!" Mandy counted them off on her fingers.

Mrs. Williams sniffed and nodded. "And what about Walton?"

Mandy looked at James. "We haven't gotten that far!"

He shrugged. "We have a little time to think of something."

"Well, I'll have to have a word with my Eric," Mrs. Williams said. But she would say no more.

So they drove off in triumph in the silver camper; cat and kittens, James, Mandy, and her grandpa.

Walton quickly regained her strength in the sunny warmth of Lilac Cottage. After three more weeks Smoky, Patch, Twinkie, and Eric began to bounce and tumble. They chased anything that moved. On Mr. Hope's lawn they sat in wait for butterflies to land on the rosebushes. Still as statues, they watched and waited. Then they bounced and pounced and tumbled. They always missed. They turned endless somersaults. Mandy would give them scores from one to ten like they were international gymnasts doing their floor exercises.

James came often to check on Eric. He lay propped on his elbows out on the lawn, with a computer magazine spread out in front of him. He pretended to read, but really he watched Eric's every move; the kitten's grumpy swipes with his front paws at mischievous Smoky and Patch, his sulking under the shade of the rhubarb leaves.

"Don't worry," Mandy said. "After a week in your house he'll be as sweet-tempered and patient as poor old Benji was. It's the Hunters' magic way with cats!"

James looked up from his magazine and smiled.

Mandy went down regularly to the village to report to Ernie on Twinkie's progress. Ernie would ask endless questions about his kitten and waited with utter impatience for the day when he could have her home. "Hey!" he warned Sammy, flipping the squirrel off his shoulder. "Stop nipping my ear, you!" The squirrel, who had free range of Ernie's kitchen, scampered down his back and around his waist, to cling on to his belt buckle.

Mandy laughed. "He'll be jealous when Twinkie comes!"

"He should be," Ernie said. "I can't wait to get that kitten home!"

At Lilac Cottage, Walton fed the four kittens less and less, watched them take to solid food, and grew rather bored with motherhood. These days she preferred a quiet corner in the kitchen underneath the vegetable bin, with a bit of peace and quiet. Her job was almost done.

Vacation time arrived. It was a green world; everyone at school was packing up and going home.

"Hey, there," Mr. Williams grunted at Mandy by

way of greeting. She was unlocking the padlock on her bike.

She glanced up. It was unusual for the custodian to talk to her at all these days, and it was weeks since she'd seen his wife. "Oh, great!" she muttered.

She hadn't forgiven him for hanging that dreadful threat over their heads, even though things had worked out fine in the end. The best she could do was to avoid the custodian whenever possible. She hastily got ready to push off for home.

"How are those kittens of yours?" Mr. Williams grumbled in his low, gravelly voice. "Getting pretty big and strong by now, I should think?"

Mandy nodded.

"And I hear you've found folk willing to take them," he persisted. One hand was on his precious garden gate, but he looked like a man with something on his mind.

Oh, go away, just go away! Mandy thought to herself.

But instead he said, "Come here a second," and looked around furtively at the lace curtains of the kitchen window. "I want to have a word with you!"

It involved Mandy riding back to school on the first day of her vacation. She had the basket strapped carefully to the back of her bike. *Who would have believed it?* she thought to herself as she lifted the basket, reached in, and gathered Walton gently into her arms.

"Come on, Walton, come on, girl!" she murmured.

"Shh!" said Mr. Williams, gesturing toward the porch. "This is still a secret!"

Mandy nodded and set Walton down. Immaculate, ladylike, and elegant as a model, Walton sniffed the logs, tested the doormat, pushed the door with her paw. It swung open.

"Eric?" Mrs. Williams called from inside the kitchen. Mandy grinned at the custodian. Then, "Eric!" Mrs. Williams said again, her voice high-pitched and surprised. "Eric, this cat has just walked back into this kitchen as if she owns the place!"

They went inside to see, and there was Mrs. Williams staring down at the familiar black-and-white shape. "How did she get here? Did she run away?" Mrs. Williams demanded.

Her husband gave a self-conscious little laugh. "No, as a matter of fact, Amy, I asked this young lady here to bring her back home for you!"

Mrs. Williams looked up at him, her eyes filling with tears. "Oh, Eric!"

"Yes, well!" He looked embarrassed. "I knew you were pining for the darn cat." He half turned toward Mandy. "She pestered me to death about it! She's too soft by half, my wife!"

Mandy watched Walton wrap herself around Mrs. Williams's legs, purring like mad. She peered in her corner for food and looked up as if to say, "Where is it?" They laughed, gave her a saucer of milk, and made a great fuss of her homecoming.

"And will we take her with us?" Mrs. Williams asked, still unable to believe her husband's change of heart.

"Why, where are you going?" Mandy asked.

"Eric's leaving his job."

"He's not . . . ?" Mandy looked anxiously at the old couple. Had Mr. Williams's arthritis finally beaten him?

"No, he hasn't been fired," Mrs. Williams said. "No, in fact the headmaster only wanted to see him to ask him to stay on beyond retirement age. He said he'd never find another custodian as good as Eric!"

Mr. Williams tut-tutted.

"Yes, he did, Eric! But he came home and we talked about it, and we decided of our own accord that we'd call it a day. We're getting on, and we want some peace and quiet in our old age."

Mr. Williams nodded. He watched Walton grooming herself after her drink. She was sitting on the windowsill, using her front paw to clean behind her ears. "Well!" he said, taken aback.

"I told you they're nice clean animals!" Mandy laughed.

"So we've decided to retire!" Mrs. Williams announced. "We've got our eye on one of the new houses just up the road!"

"A quiet little street, plenty of garden!" Mr. Williams said.

"Perfect for Walton?" Mandy could hardly keep the smile from spreading all over her face.

The custodian looked at his wife and broke into a grin. "I suppose so," he said, shaking his head.

"And will it be all right if I make an appointment at Animal Ark for Walton's operation?" Mandy asked, trying to be tactful.

"Operation?" Mr. Williams repeated slowly.

"Yes, so she won't have any more kittens."

"Oh," he said, very old-fashioned. "*That* operation!"

"Yes, you don't want any more little ones cluttering up your kitchen, getting into your best shirts!"

Mr. Williams turned bright red. He looked sheepishly at his wife, then his face broke into a broad grin again. "I should say not!" he agreed.

So Mandy made the arrangements. She wouldn't hear of them having to pay for Walton being spayed. She knew her mom and dad would want that, too. So she said she would schedule Walton for the following Monday. Mandy took the hand offered by Mr. Williams and shook it warmly.

"No hard feelings?" he asked.

"None!" she said.

Mandy rode home along the field road. She felt on top of the world. The road crested the hill. Lapwings curved overhead in the clear sky, the fields rolled in every direction. Perfect!

She headed downhill to Welford and Animal Ark. She'd go in to see who else needed rescuing; maybe a lost hedgehog who'd found its way to the examining room or a "male" hamster who'd just produced six babies! ("The pet shop said it was a boy, they did really!")

The wind caught Mandy's hair. She tilted her head back and stuck her legs out sideways to freewheel down the hill. And she laughed out loud.

ANIMAL ARK®
Where animals come first

Look for Animal Ark®:
DOLPHIN IN THE DEEP

The red sun was low in the sky. It cast a pink glow over the white houses of Dixie Springs as Mandy, Joel, and Mel picked their way between the rows of sponges set out along the dock.

"Can we take a boat out?" Joel asked. They'd finished their chocolate chip ice cream and were taking a stroll along the pier, looking for dolphins. There was just time to do a circuit of the bay before the sun sank out of sight.

"Sure." Mel seemed to have his mind on other things. "You and Mandy go. I'll wait here."

"Is that okay?" Mandy checked. Mel still looked

worried. "You don't want to go back and find out how Bob is?"

Mel smiled. "No, you go ahead." He spoke to a fisherman who was working in his boat, and fixed up a quick trip for Mandy and Joel. "See you!" he called. "Watch out for those dolphins. Steve Peratinos here will take you to the best places. He keeps a log. Ask him."

Soon they set off and curved across the still water toward the setting sun. Their fisherman was a friendly old man with strong, wiry arms and broad hands that gripped the wheel. He wore a faded denim cap, and his face was lined from years in the sun.

"What kind of log do you keep?" Mandy asked. Every ripple in the sea's smooth surface promised a dolphin sighting, but so far they hadn't been lucky.

"I write down how many dolphins I see, what they do, which direction they swim in. Stuff like that." Steve Peratinos swung the boat around toward the far shore. "We set up a Dolphin Watch last year."

"Who's we?" Joel asked. The breeze blew through his T-shirt and against the peak of his cap, so he decided to turn it around and wear it back to front.

"Guys who fish around here. And the Coast Guard, a couple of scientists from Orlando . . . you know." Steve's deep, gravelly voice drifted on. "The best time is around spring, when they have their young. That's when the count shoots way up!"

"I guess we missed it." Joel moved restlessly around the edge of the boat, peering down.

"Over there!" Mandy pointed to an area close to the shore. She'd spotted dolphins.

Steve altered course. "Yeah, you missed that part," he explained, "but the young calves are still around. You might get lucky."

"We already did." Mandy pointed again. Two dolphins had risen to the surface close by — a mother and her offspring by the look of things. "Isn't that great?"

She saw how the calf shadowed its mother, rising for air then diving out of sight. Then there were more dolphins, weaving through the bow wave of their boat, playing in the spray. "How old is the calf?" she asked.

"Four months, maybe five."

"It's quite big already." The calf was almost as long as its mother, but much thinner.

"How long do they stay together?"

"Mother and calf? Let's see. The young guy won't leave her side until he's six months old. Then he'll go off to catch a few fish. But he won't be weaned until he's a year and a half old."

"Wow! Did you see that?" Joel shot across the boat to

the far side. "Three of them jumping way out. Did you see it?"

"Sit down, you're rocking the boat!" Steve warned him, then he went on explaining to Mandy about the young calf. "He feeds on milk, just like you and me."

Mandy frowned. "Underwater?"

Steve laughed. "It's kind of neat. Mom has a slit in her belly. When she wants to feed the baby, out pops the nipple."

"P-lease!" Joel cried, pretending to cover his ears.

Steve went on. "And the calf's tongue kind of makes a tube when he presses it against the roof of his mouth. He puts his mouth to the nipple, Mom squirts milk into the tube, and there you go. One pretty neat system, hey?"

"Amazing!" Mandy marveled. Another mystery solved.

"Hey!" Steve cried, as Joel ignored their conversation and flung himself back across the boat for a better view of the acrobatic dolphins. "Steady!"

But the warning came too late. The boat rocked from Joel's reckless leap. He overbalanced and tried to catch hold of the rail.

"Grab him!" Steve yelled at Mandy. "He's going over!"

She lunged and touched Joel's fingertips as the boat tilted and he slipped away, across the wet deck. The next second, he was gone.

Springing into action, Steve cut the engine. "Man overboard! Can you see him?"

Over the side, down in the deep blue water, there was a froth of bubbles rising to the surface, but no sign of Joel himself. "No! He's gone under!" cried Mandy.

The three playful dolphins gave up their game and vanished. Four or five others swam quietly nearby.

It was as if time stood still. Mandy stared down at the rising bubbles, stunned by what had happened.

Then Steve unhitched the lifebelt and threw it into the water. "Did he hit his head?" he yelled at Mandy.

"I don't know. It happened too quick." She was kicking off her shoes, ready to jump into the sea. Someone had to dive down there and see.

"Hold it!" Steve was there beside her, holding on to her arm. The boat still bobbed dangerously. He didn't want a second emergency if Mandy were to leap out into danger.

She strained to get free. "Please!" she begged. "He could drown!"

Sarah—

Some of these are
bizarrely ridiculous—
others fit us well

Love you
Mom

mothers &
daughters

THAT SPECIAL BOND

Compiled by Suzanne Beilenson

PETER PAUPER PRESS, INC.
White Plains, New York

For my own wonderful mother,
Evelyn Loeb Beilenson

Designed by Heather Zschock
Photographs copyright © 2008 Corbis
Butterflies artwork by Ann Johnstone for Jane Mosse Designs

Visit us at www.peterpauper.com

mothers &
daughters

THAT SPECIAL BOND

CONTENTS

Introduction 6

Daughters Talk about Their Mothers 8

What Mothers Say about Their Daughters 48

The Mother-Daughter Relationship 65

In search of my mother's garden — (Beware of dog poo)
I found my own.

—ALICE WALKER

INTRODUCTION

*A*t any given moment, she is your best friend, your closest confidante, your mirror image, or even the bane of your existence. No matter what, though, she is always the most important woman in your life. She is your mother. She is your daughter.

There is no other relationship quite as special as the one between a mother and her daughter. A daughter learns her first lessons at her mother's knee. As a girl grows, her mother is her role model for becoming a woman. She will imitate that image, co-opt that image, and maybe even rebel against it, but it is always her mother who defines the standard.

Likewise, a mother learns just as much from her daughter. She sees the best of herself in her daughter, and sometimes the not-so-best. A mother always has hopes and dreams for her daughter. Yet, in growing up, a daughter's life can fulfill those ideals or simply baffle her mother. Always, though, a daughter opens new horizons for her mother, shows her the unending possibilities of the world, the changes that come with the times, and new definitions of being a woman.

As you'll see from the quotations in this book, the bond between a mother and daughter is one of the strongest in each of their lives. The love between them is a rock in the often turbulent waters of life. They are women standing together—learning, living, and, most of all, loving.

—S. B.

Daughters

TALK ABOUT THEIR

Mothers

I'm able to write about a good
mother because I had a good mother—
unequivocally. She was quite different
than I am. . . . I'm a somewhat driven,
ambitious person, very interested in an
intellectual life. My mother wasn't like that.
She was quieter and more reserved than
I am. . . . She had a vested interest in
making us feel good. At the time,
I took it for granted that that's how
mothers were, and now I just thank
God almost every day.

—ANNA QUINDLEN

*My mother thought it's
always a good idea not to
buy things for people,
but to either learn something
from memory or do
something with my hands.
That has more value than
something you buy.*

—CAROLINE KENNEDY

I often think of my mother.
Though I do not remember what
she looked like, I feel her presence
with me all the time. I still
feel her warmth, her beauty…

—EARTHA KITT

MAMA EXHORTED HER CHILDREN AT
EVERY OPPORTUNITY TO "JUMP AT DE SUN."
WE MIGHT NOT LAND ON THE SUN,
BUT AT LEAST WE WOULD GET
OFF THE GROUND.

—ZORA NEALE HURSTON

*I pray that I may be all that
my mother would have been, had
she lived in an age when women
could aspire and achieve.*

—RUTH BADER GINSBURG, *Supreme Court Justice*

*Although my mother and I were nothing alike,
I realized that I was her girl more than I had ever been
my father's. She had made me stand out from other girls,
had dressed me, had taught me to sing, had let me quit school. (not)
And now she was encouraging me to grow up ...*

—GLORIA SWANSON

…I think I always got a little thrill standing backstage, and listening or watching, especially if it was a song that I knew and loved. But she also— all the members of my family made a real effort, and especially mom, to keep things as—quote-unquote—"normal" as possible, I think, at home. And so— she was always there at breakfast, which was an amazing thing, given her schedule.

—EMMA WALTON HAMILTON,
daughter of Julie Andrews

When Jimmy Carter was President, he called and said, "Loretta, we want you to come up here. Five famous people will come in and bring the teacher that has taught 'em the most." . . . So I told President Carter I couldn't bring a teacher. And he said, "Why?" I said, "Well, my mommy was what taught me most." And he said, "Well, there's always got to be a first. Bring her." That was the biggest thrill that my mother ever had.

—Loretta Lynn

She is the parent I remember and
hers is the life I keep mining for gold,
running my sieve through the same old
streams, searching for precious nuggets
that might connect my memories of
her to the life I have lived without her.
I keep hoping that the missing pieces
will turn up in my mother's past.

—LETTY COTTIN POGREBIN

*She's my teacher, my adviser,
my greatest inspiration.*

—WHITNEY HOUSTON

*Mother came from a self-supporting family,
where work was work and play was work.
If any of us weren't good at what we were being
taught (as I wasn't at painting), those lessons ended.
Her overwhelming belief in us didn't blind her...
and that's probably one very good reason why
I was able to become what I became.*

—SUZANNE FARRELL

Always I heard Mother's emotional voice asking Amy and me and our **younger sister, Molly, the same few** questions: Is that your own idea? Or somebody else's? . . . She herself held many unpopular, even fantastic, positions. Opposition emboldened her, and she would take on anybody on any issue.

—Annie Dillard

She has always been there for me," says Kate of her mother. "The single most frustrating thing about fame, when you are a child, is sitting opposite your mother in a restaurant and having people come up. You might be in the middle of something really important and then Mom is suddenly asked for an autograph. Some people can be rude and intrusive at times, but watching Mom deal with it was a lesson for life. She was always polite and warm."

—Kate Hudson

*It was my mother, however, who taught me
the rituals of prayer. She took her faith very seriously.
No matter where she was in the world, or what
she was doing, she prostrated herself five times
a day in prayer. When I was nine years old,
she began to include me, slipping into my
bedroom to lead me in the morning prayer.
Together we would perform the* wuzoo,
*the washing of our hands, feet, and faces so that
we would be pure before God, then prostrate
ourselves facing west toward Mecca.*

—BENAZIR BHUTTO

yes, lots
of this

MOMMA WAS HOME. SHE WAS THE MOST
TOTALLY HUMAN, HUMAN BEING THAT I HAVE EVER KNOWN;
AND SO VERY BEAUTIFUL. SHE WAS THE LIGHTHOUSE
OF HER COMMUNITY. WITHIN OUR HOME, SHE WAS
AN ABUNDANCE OF LOVE, DISCIPLINE, FUN, AFFECTION,
STRENGTH, TENDERNESS, ENCOURAGEMENT,
UNDERSTANDING, INSPIRATION, SUPPORT.

—LEONTYNE PRICE

*I hear my mother when I'm being
my best self—soothing someone else....
My mother's big message was that you
take care of other people ...*

—COKIE ROBERTS

One of my earliest memories is of my mother...
setting aside dollars for the specific charity requests
that touched them. She taught me that I had an
obligation to give something back to society,
no matter how little that could be some months.

—ALI MACGRAW

THE FIRST TIME I REALIZED I HAD BECOME
MY MOTHER WAS WHEN I MOVED INTO MY
NEW APARTMENT. IT HAS THIS AMAZING,
FULLY EQUIPPED KITCHEN—
AND I ORDERED IN CHINESE FOOD.
I'M THE WORST COOK EVER—
JUST LIKE MY MOTHER.

—RICKI LAKE

I COULDN'T HAVE A BETTER FRIEND THAN MY MOTHER.
I NEVER HAD TO BE AFRAID TO TALK TO HER ABOUT ANYTHING. . . .
AND THE BASIC THINGS THAT MY MOTHER TAUGHT ME
ARE PRETTY MUCH RIGHT ON. BUT SHE NEVER RESTRICTED ME. . . .
IF I WANTED TO DO SOMETHING THAT SHE DIDN'T APPROVE OF
SHE'D SAY, "WELL, I USUALLY TELL YOU HOW IT IS.
IF YOU WANT TO GO AHEAD AND DO THIS, IT'S UP TO YOU.
BUT JUST KNOW THAT I DON'T APPROVE."

—LACY J. DALTON

When my mother had to get dinner
for eight she'd just make enough
for sixteen and only serve half.

—GRACIE ALLEN

My mom buys things I wouldn't wear in a million years.

—CHASTITY BONO, *daughter of Cher*

This is very true.

My mother looked to me like a fairy princess,
far too beautiful to be a Mom—a fair, rare creature
who lived in a magic kingdom. I always entered her
dressing room as if drawn into a dream. Her domain was
draped in ice-blue taffeta sprinkled with violets and
sparkled with antique silver, Venetian glass, and tiny
enameled boxes. Only a princess belonged here,
not a six-year-old with clumsy hands.

—CANDICE BERGEN

THERE WAS A HEMLOCK TREE ON THE WEST SIDE
OF THE PROPERTY. THAT WAS THE TREE I USED TO CLIMB.
THE NEIGHBORS USED TO CALL MOTHER.
"KIT! KATHY IS IN THE TOP OF THE HEMLOCK!"
"YES, I KNOW. DON'T SCARE HER. SHE DOESN'T
KNOW THAT IT'S DANGEROUS."

—KATHARINE HEPBURN

My mother told me I was dancing
before I was born. She could feel my toes
tapping wildly inside her for months.

—GINGER ROGERS

When she was with us,
her time was entirely ours.
She never went out to dinner
or had a friend to visit.
She was totally ours.

—ISABELLA ROSSELLINI

"And I mean it!" is the phrase my mother
used when she really wanted me to do something.
Now I tell my daughter Ellie, "Get out of the bathtub—
and I mean it." The other day, I overheard
Ellie [age 2-1/2] in the playground, bossing around
the other little kids: *"And I mean it!"*

—Katie Couric

My mother used to have an expression:
"There's only one woman around
this house—and it's me!"

—Naomi Campbell

I miss thee, my Mother!
Thy image is still
The deepest impressed
on my heart.

—ELIZA COOK

Now that I am in my forties, she tells me I'm beautiful;
now that I am in my forties, she sends me presents
and we have the long, personal and even remarkably
honest phone calls I always wanted so intensely I forbade
myself to imagine them. How strange.... I am deeply grateful.
With my poems, I finally won even my mother.
The longest wooing of my life.

—MARGE PIERCY

When we weren't scratching each other's eyes out, we were making each other laugh harder than anyone else could.

—LUCIE ARNAZ,
working with her mother on I Love Lucy

I was supposed to be just like her;
I was supposed to fight with everyone to prove
that I was one of the strong ones too.

—B. D. HYMAN, *on her mother, Bette Davis*

When Mother taught us the Lord's Prayer,
she put her heart into it. You tried to say it as she did,
and you had to put a little of your own heart into it.
I believe that Mother, realizing that she was left alone
to raise three girls, knew that she had to
have a support beyond herself.

—MARIAN ANDERSON

When I first started entertainin', Mama would say,
"Now, Reba, your jokes are real cute,
but just quit talkin' and sing." . . .
God put me on this earth to sing.
Basically He gave the voice first to Mama.
But Mama couldn't use it, so she passed it down
to us kids. So that's how it worked out.

—Reba McEntire

*No matter how perfect your mother thinks you are,
she will always want to fix your hair.*

—Suzanne Beilenson

The "to-do" list

*Two years ago, a friend commented
to me about how many lists I made
and how many little yellow stick-'ems I leave
around the house to remind myself of things.
At that moment it dawned on me that
I had become . . . Joan Rivers!*

—MELISSA RIVERS

And it came to me, and I knew
what I had to have before my soul
would rest. I wanted to belong—
to belong to my mother. And in return—
I wanted my mother to belong to me.

—GLORIA VANDERBILT

I AM LENA'S DAUGHTER. MY DAUGHTERS ARE
HER GRANDDAUGHTERS. FAMILY FACES ARE MAGIC MIRRORS.
LOOKING AT PEOPLE WHO BELONG TO US,
WE SEE THE PAST, PRESENT, AND FUTURE.

—GAIL HORNE JONES LUMET

My mother told me stories all the time. . . .
And in all of those stories she told me
who I was, who I was supposed to be,
whom I came from, and who would follow me.
In this way, she taught me the meaning of
the words she said, that all life is a circle
and everything has a place within it.

—Paula Gunn Allen

To describe my mother would
be to write about a hurricane in
its perfect power. Or the climbing,
falling colors of a rainbow.

—Maya Angelou

I ALSO LEARNED FROM MY MOTHER THE JOY OF WRITING.
SEEING YOUR STORY UNFOLD AND YOUR CHARACTERS DEVELOP.
WE SOMETIMES READ EACH OTHER'S WORKS IN
PROGRESS AND TALK TO EACH OTHER ABOUT IT.

—CAROL HIGGINS CLARK

The first time I heard my mother's
voice come out of my mouth was
when I started yelling at my sisters,
"Clean up after yourselves!"
It's something my mother said—
and now I can't help but say it too.

—Christy Turlington

Dear Mother: I'm all right.
Stop worrying about me.

—Papyrus letter of 17-year-old
Egyptian girl, ca. 2000 b.c.

44

MY MOTHER WAS THE MOTHER OF THE WORLD.
SHE'D CORRECT PEOPLE'S MANNERS AND
MORALS WITHOUT EVEN KNOWING THEM.
IT WASN'T UNTIL I GREW UP THAT I REALLY
UNDERSTOOD HOW GREAT A WOMAN SHE WAS—
HER HIGH STANDARDS, STRICT DISCIPLINE,
GOOD MANNERS, WORK HABITS. I LEARNED
FROM HER THAT WHEN YOU MOP A FLOOR,
YOU GET DOWN ON YOUR HANDS AND KNEES
TO GET INTO THE CORNERS.

—DEE DEE BELLSON, *daughter of Pearl Bailey*

*I wish you would mention the joy
she had for life. That's what she gave me.
If she was the tragic figure they said she was,
I would be a wreck, wouldn't I? . . .
She lived eight lives in one, and yet
I thought she would outlive us all.
She was a great talent and for the rest
of my life, I will be proud to be
Judy Garland's daughter.*

—LIZA MINNELLI

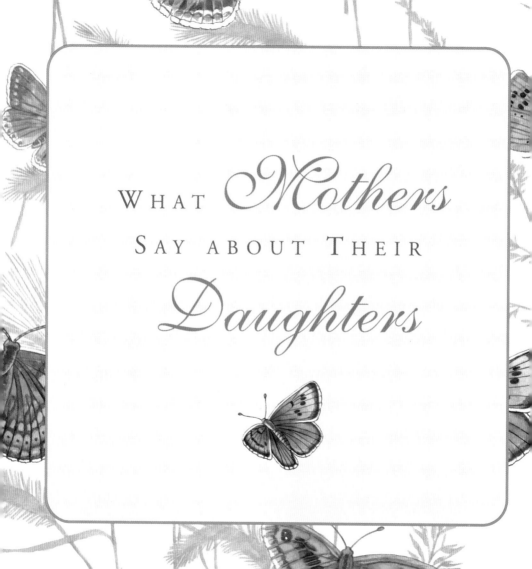

WHAT *Mothers*

SAY ABOUT THEIR

Daughters

My daughter's birth was the incomparable gift of seeing the world at quite a different angle than before, and judging it by standards that would apply far beyond my natural life.

—Alice Walker

I love my daughter. She and I have shared my body. There is a part of her mind that is a part of mine. But when she was born, she sprang from me like a slippery fish, and has been swimming away ever since.

—Amy Tan

Gwynnie is her own person.
When we talk, I feel as if I've been
invited to a secret place of hers.
It makes those times that were
difficult worthwhile.

—BLYTHE DANNER, *mother of Gwyneth Paltrow*

I WAS PREGNANT WHEN I DID THE FIRST SHOT OF *PROOF*,
AND I STARTED TO SHOW BY THE END. IT WAS VERY IMPORTANT
TO ME TO TAKE SOME TIME TO BE WITH MYSELF AND MY
FAMILY AND TAKE IT EASY AND ENJOY BEING PREGNANT.
WHEN I HAD MY DAUGHTER, I JUST FELL IN LOVE WITH HER,
SO THEN I WAS RETICENT ABOUT LEAVING HER AS A
TINY BABY AND GOING BACK TO WORK.

—GWYNETH PALTROW, *talking about her daughter, Apple*

As I look back on my early years of parenthood,
one thing I regret is the amount of time I spent
looking ahead toward my children's next big step.
When they were born, I waited for them to smile.
When they smiled, I watched for them to sit up.
Not that I didn't take pleasure in the moment.
But so much of raising children is about forward
movement and growth. And, especially
with a first child, ... you know so little of the
road ahead that you're always anticipating
what's around the corner.

—Joyce Maynard

I think it is important to convey to my daughter, who is five, a sense of possibilities about her place in the world. We've taught her to aspire to life in a world that is gender-neutral, and at the same time have encouraged her to challenge things not in keeping with that vision.

—SUSAN G. COLE

WE'RE COMPLETELY TYPICAL. I GET MY FEELINGS HURT.
I PUSH THE GIRLS' BUTTONS. I INSTALLED THEM—
I CERTAINLY KNOW HOW TO PUSH THEM! NEVERTHELESS,
MY RELATIONSHIP WITH WY AND ASHLEY IS HEALTHIER
THAN THE ONE I HAVE WITH MY MOM.
WE HAVE BOUNDARIES—THAT'S BECAUSE WE'VE
BEEN IN THERAPY. AND OUR RELATIONSHIP IS MUCH
MORE EXPRESSIVE. I LOVE THEM SO DEEPLY.

—NAOMI JUDD

I never thought that I was very maternal but I just loved Melanie so much and enjoyed being with her. She's so happy now— and I'm so happy for her.

—TIPPI HEDREN, *Melanie Griffith's mother*

Sound familiar?

It's such a shock when your child turns into a wild thing. When you've had a storybook child, and all of a sudden, you get the Exorcist. You walk in the room and see a green face with a tongue sticking out, saying, "I hate you!"

—LEE GRANT, *mother of Dinah Manoff*

WHAT I CELEBRATE ABOUT MY DAUGHTER IS
HER FRANKNESS, HER FEISTINESS,
HER TWIN ABILITIES TO HAVE HER EYES
FLOOD WITH TEARS AND APPLY EYELINER
FAR BETTER THAN I EVER DID.

—PHYLLIS THEROUX

*It's important for me that
my daughters see that whether
I win or lose, I can always stand
up for what I believe.*

—ESTHER SHAPIRO

*Melissa is the one to whom
I could give total affection and feel
it being absorbed and returned.*

—JOAN RIVERS

*I knew what was important
for me and that a successful
career would mean nothing
without a personal life.
So the children would
always be with me.*

—JANET LEIGH

THE
Mother-
Daughter
RELATIONSHIP

When a mother finally decides
to give her daughter some advice,
the mother usually learns plenty.

—EVAN ESAR

*Every one can keep House better
than her Mother, till she trieth.*

—THOMAS FULLER

Marry the daughter on
knowing the mother.

—HINDU PROVERB

The daughter of a busy mother
makes a bad housekeeper.

—IRISH PROVERB

*The first child of a woman of good
blood is always a girl.*

—ITALIAN PROVERB

O more beautiful daughter
of a beautiful mother.

—HORACE

*I'm more a mom than I am a celebrity,
even though I know you know me
as a celebrity. I'm a mother first.*

—DIANA ROSS

*For a mother, sending your first child to college means
learning to let go. I believe this is especially true when the
child you're packing off is a daughter. The sense of identification
is so much stronger than it is with a son. You can remember
yourself as a young woman leaving home for school, the
exhilaration and uncertainty of entering a new phase of life.
But if going away to college is a rite of passage for a child,
it is equally so for a mother.*

—JANE FONDA

Our mothers are our most direct
connection to our history and our gender.

—HOPE EDELMAN

WHAT *DO* GIRLS DO WHO HAVEN'T ANY MOTHERS
TO HELP THEM THROUGH THEIR TROUBLES?

—LOUISA MAY ALCOTT

*Even though we rarely agree on anything, I have loved her
longer than anyone in my lifetime. Our relationship began the
day of my conception and has already lasted a half-century; it is,
furthermore, the only truly unconditional love—neither one's
children nor one's most fervent lovers love in that way.*

—ISABEL ALLENDE

YOU NEVER GET OVER BEING A CHILD, LONG
AS YOU HAVE A MOTHER TO GO TO.

—SARAH ORNE JEWETT

Children are apt to live up to what you believe of them.

—LADY BIRD JOHNSON